Ice Storm

Ice
Storm

Penny Draper

WILLOWS
ELEMENTARY SCHOOL

COTEAU
BOOKS
FOR KIDS

Edited by Barbara Sapergia
Cover painting by Aries Cheung
Cover design by Tom Dart
Book design by Duncan Campbell
Typeset by Susan Buck
Printed and bound in Canada by Houghton Boston

Library and Archives Canada Cataloguing in Publication

Draper, Penny, 1957-
    Ice storm / Penny Draper.

(Disaster strikes; 6)
ISBN 978-1-55050-451-4

    I. Title. II. Series: Draper, Penny, 1957- . Disaster strikes ; 6.

PS8607.R36I34 2011   jC813'.6   C2011-900759-2

Library of Congress Control Number: 2011921841

2517 Victoria Avenue
Regina, Saskatchewan
Canada S4P 0T2
www.coteaubooks.com

Available in Canada from:
Publishers Group Canada
2440 Viking Way
Richmond, British Columbia
Canada V6V 1N2

Available in the US from:
Orca Book Publishers
www.orcabook.com
1-800-210-5277

10 9 8 7 6 5 4 3 2 1

Coteau Books gratefully acknowledges the financial support of its publishing program by: the Saskatchewan Arts Board, the Canada Council for the Arts, the Government of Canada through the Canada Book Fund, the Government of Saskatchewan through the Creative Economy Entrepreneurial Fund and the City of Regina Arts Commission.

 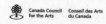

To Shirley and Ken of Hillandale Farm
and the dairy farmers who put milk on our tables

and to Aunt Margaret,

who always had a tin of my favourite cookies
waiting when I came to visit the farm

CONTENTS

ALICE

ALICE HATED HER ALARM CLOCK.

It had been such a lovely dream. She'd been skating, flying over the ice. Only her mother was watching; there was not a frowning judge anywhere. As her dream self gathered speed for the double axel, she'd felt absolute confidence deep inside. The landing was magic. Her mother's smile lit up the arena.

Then the alarm's shrill scream ruined everything, pushing her mother's face back into the fog of sleep. It was 5:00 a.m.

Alice burrowed a little deeper under the covers. Having to give up her warm bed for a cold arena made her want to cry. But her skating pro would be waiting. And the junior Canadian championships were just around the corner.

Alice had to skate all the time. It wasn't fun any more.

Trouble was, everyone said she was a great figure skater. A real star. So she *had* to skate, and too bad if it took every waking moment. Her dad did his part. He had to work long hours because ice time and skating pros cost a lot of money. They both kept doing it because it would have made her mother happy. That should have made it worth the effort, but Alice knew she was unhappy. No time, no life, no friends. Except for one – her cousin Sophie, who lived on a dairy farm near Saint-Hyacinthe. Sophie didn't get to Montréal very often, although they emailed each other every day. Thank goodness for Sophie.

They hadn't always been friends. Their moms were sisters and thought the girls should be close because they were exactly the same age. But they'd never liked one another, not even when they were small. They were complete opposites. Dark and light. Tall and short. City and country. They didn't even speak the same first language, because Sophie's mom had married a francophone man and their family spoke French most of the time. When the families visited, Alice and Sophie always got pushed together, whether they liked it or not.

Sophie hadn't been interested in anything Alice had to say about the city and she'd thought it was funny that Alice knew nothing about life on a farm. And she'd been completely unimpressed by Alice's skating.

But all that had been three years ago, before Alice's

mom died. Everything was different now.

Alice pulled her underwear and tights from beneath the covers at the bottom of her bed where they kept nice and warm. Sophie had taught her that. Scrunching down so that she was completely under the blanket, Alice made a small volcano as she wiggled into her bottom layer of practice clothes. Then she jumped out of bed and pulled on warm-up clothes over the tights. Next came her sweats.

Almost ready to brave the cold outside, Alice took a minute to check her email. Soph had come through with her morning message. She had to get up as early as Alice to help with the cows.

Sébastien went to a sleepover the other night and they told scary stories. Now he is sure that a *loup-garou* is coming. As if werewolves even existed! Yesterday he didn't even know what one was. Now he thinks a monster is just waiting to bite him and change his life forever. He doesn't even know if he should be excited or afraid and Alice, he's always talking about it, even at school! I could just die of embarrassment. First time he's ever been invited anywhere and it's a disaster! Maman says she's never letting him go to a sleepover again. Love Soph.

Alice laughed out loud.

Sébastien was Sophie's little brother, a genius and a complete weirdo. He had these spooky green eyes that stared right into Alice's brain, and he said things that made her think he actually came from another planet. Sébastien's school said that he was "special" – too smart for the regular world. His report cards always had stuff like "needs constant challenge" and "unable to socialize with his peers." He worried her Aunt Evie and Uncle Henri. But the grown-ups didn't get that everything Sébastien said made perfect sense after you got past the weird part. He was just a little freaky. Sophie complained about him all the time but Alice wouldn't have minded having Sébastien as her little brother. He practically was anyway.

Alice went downstairs, collected her gear from the mudroom and headed to the car. It was raining. Perfect. It should be snowing in January, for heaven's sake. Dad had the car warming up, sending great swirls of white exhaust to dance against the black sky. Alice slid in the front, hunkering down into the heated seat. Sweet. Dad had traded in his old car to get the heated seats, just for her. They were great, especially on a below-zero morning like today.

How on earth could it rain?

They didn't talk much so early in the morning, not until they reached St-Viateur Bagels. The shop had their order ready: three black-seed and three white-seed. It was Mom who'd started the bagel tradition. The St-Viateur folks filled up Dad's thermos with coffee and the two of them were back on the road, eating their first bagels straight from the bag, plain and hot. After that they were awake enough to chat about skating, school, Dad's job at the power company, just stuff. Nothing important.

When they got to the rink they both ate another bagel, this time with cream cheese and a cup of coffee from the thermos. Dad always brought milk and sugar to add to Alice's cup. Mom would never have allowed it, so it was kind of like a secret even though, well, it really didn't matter any more. The last two bagels were for her coach, Mr. Osborne. He was waiting, as usual. He was never late. It if weren't for the fact that the routine had to start at 5:00 a.m., Alice could almost have enjoyed the quiet morning time.

Alice started her practice. Dad stayed to finish his coffee and read the newspaper. Then he came to the boards to give her a quick hug before he left for work. As soon as he left, Alice tackled her double axel. Sure, it was a hard jump. It was an extra half-revolution more than the other double jumps, and you had to take off going forward instead of backward, and you couldn't use your toe pick to help you get into the air. But hard didn't bother Alice. She landed it over and over and over again. It was easy in practice. She just couldn't land it in competition. Ever.

As usual, the practice went on too long. The taxi that took her to school was waiting, and she was late for school. But she never got in trouble: the teachers seemed to think she was some sort of celebrity or something. As if. The rest of the kids never noticed. To them, she didn't even exist.

The competition was so close. Alice's nerves were already beginning to flare. She barely made it through her classes. She just couldn't concentrate and was grateful when two o'clock came. That's when the taxi came to take her back to the rink for four more hours of practice. Then Dad arrived to pick her up. Practice, practice, practice. She wished the judges would come and watch her, judge her, in secret. She didn't want to have to see them. Then they'd find out what she could really do.

SOPHIE

SOPHIE STRETCHED, LOVING THE WARMTH OF HER bed. She reached down between the covers to grab her warm housecoat and socks, then braced herself for the moment when she had to get out of bed. The cold air in her bedroom always made her shrink inside her skin, forcing her to run all the way to the warmth of the kitchen.

"Sophie, are you up?" called her mother.

"I'm up!" she shouted back, and smiled as she thought of the big wood stove in the kitchen and the cup of *chocolat chaud* that would be waiting for her. Winter in Québec wasn't so bad, not if you could wake up to a wood stove and hot chocolate, and maybe even pancakes and maple syrup.

Maman *had* made pancakes. Sébastien was already inhaling a stack that was as big as his head.

"Petit cochon!" Sophie said under her breath. Nine-

year-old Sébastien just stared at her, and squeezed another huge forkful into his mouth. His dark hair stood up in crazy spikes all over his head. She hoped Maman would make him comb it flat before he went to school. He wouldn't if she didn't make him. Sophie gave Maman a kiss, then sat down.

"Where's Papa?"

"In the barn," replied Maman.

Sophie stood up suddenly. "Is it Adalie?" she asked, worried.

"Oui, but sit down," replied Maman in a calm voice. "There's no problem. Papa is just being careful."

Adalie was one of Sophie's favourite cows. The last time she had given birth there had been a lot of trouble. The baby calf died and Adalie nearly had as well. This time, all seemed to be going well, but anything could happen when a cow gave birth.

"May I stay home to help? *S'il te plaît?* Papa might need me," pleaded Sophie. Staying home, of course, had the added bonus of a day without the embarrassment of Sébastien's constant search for the *loup-garou.*

"Non," said Maman. "Papa has called the vet, who will come if needed. It's his job. Your job is to go to school. Don't you want to see your friends?"

Sophie sighed. Her friends could wait. She really wanted to be there when Adalie had her calf. But if Maman said no, that was no. Sophie wasn't the kind of girl who argued with her parents. She didn't like to make a commotion. She chose to show her disappointment in other ways, like leaving her breakfast dishes on the table and fighting with Sébastien. But Maman barely noticed Sophie's small rebellions.

By the time Sébastien finally finished his logger's-size plate of pancakes, they were late. Even so, he made Sophie wait until he found his new video camera, a gift from Christmas.

"Why do you need it at school?" demanded Sophie with exasperation. *"Viens-toi!"* The two of them pulled on their snow gear and walked to the end of the lane to wait for the school bus.

"I think there is a *loup-garou* at school, in the cupboard where the basketballs are stored. I'm going to film it. I will take its soul so it cannot hurt me," explained Sébastien. Sophie just groaned. Why was it that she had to get stuck with a brother like him? Some days, Sophie was more than willing to let Alice have Sébastien for her very own. Days like today.

Sophie tried to hurry Sébastien down the drive. If she had to go to school, then she didn't want to miss the bus. But Sébastien would not be hurried.

"Will Adalie's calf have a soul?" Sébastien asked.

"What?!" Sophie frowned at her brother.

"If this calf dies too, will it go to heaven? Will it be the same heaven as we go to?"

"Sébastien, that's awful! The calf won't die." Sophie shook her head in disgust.

"What if it does?" worried Sébastien. "Or maybe Adalie will die instead. How old do you have to be to have a soul? Are there different heavens for mothers and fathers and children, or is there just one place for everybody?"

Sophie rolled her eyes. "How am I supposed to know? Why are we even talking about this? It's stupid! You're crazy, *c'est sûr.*" She frowned. "No animals are going to die."

Sébastien stared at his sister for a moment. Then he looked up. "It's raining," he said.

Sophie huddled deeper into her hood. "It's not supposed to rain in January," she grumbled.

"You should have told Maman how much you wanted to stay home. She would have listened," said Sébastien.

"What?" Sébastien's constant changes of subject made Sophie dizzy sometimes. "Tell Maman what?"

"You never tell her what you really want. How's she supposed to know?"

Sophie just stared at her little brother. He didn't say another word until the school bus came and he took his lonely seat at the front of the bus. As Sophie passed him on the way to the back where her friends sat, she looked at him quizzically. He was so strange. His brain bounced around all over the place, but then he would come out with something that proved he'd been paying attention all along. She would never understand him.

Alice was better at that. Alice got Sébastien in a way that Sophie just couldn't. Sophie sighed. She wasn't sure she'd tell Alice what he'd said. It sounded like a criticism, and criticism she kept close to her heart. The bad stuff wasn't for sharing.

Anyway, thought Sophie, shaking off her brother's weirdness for the millionth time, Alice had her own problems right now. The competition was so close. Sophie was in awe of Alice's ability to perform in front of all those people, the TV cameras and the judges. She couldn't do it in a thousand years. Deep down, Sophie had to admit that Alice wasn't really very good at performing either, but, she thought loyally, at least her cousin tried. Alice was a great skater, probably the best in the whole country for her age, but she got so nervous in competition that she almost always made a mess of it. That meant that she needed a lot of boosting up before the competition and a good shoulder to cry on after the competition. But Sophie didn't mind. Alice was her cousin and her best friend. She'd do anything to help her.

As the school bus jounced over the snow ruts, Sophie smiled when she thought about Alice's early visits to the farm. Alice was so beautiful and so accomplished that she'd terrified Sophie. Alice's parents had always called her "Princess," and that's sure what she looked – and acted – like. Sophie had felt fat and frumpy compared to Alice with her wavy brown hair and her fancy clothes and her TV interview voice. Sophie never knew what to say or do, or how to entertain her during the visit. Alice always seemed disgusted with everything at the farm. It had made Sophie feel embarrassed.

But when Alice's Mom was sick, Alice was so sad. She seemed to really need somebody and Sophie loved to be needed. That was when they started being friends. Thank goodness.

Sophie could tell Alice stuff by email that she would never dare tell her school friends face to face. And Alice could too. Now that they were both twelve, they were forever friends.

DAY ONE
Monday, January 5, 1998

MONTREAL TAXI DRIVERS DRIVE FAST.

Alice liked to sit in front with Guillaume, the driver who always picked her up at the rink in the morning to take her to school, then took her from school back to the rink in the afternoon. Guillaume could change lanes, squeeze through traffic and find all the green lights without ever honking the horn or touching the brakes. It was like being in a race car. And he talked non-stop the whole time. He talked about his family, his job and the other drivers on the road. Best of all, he told her stories. Stories of old Québec, of the *loup-garou* and the Flying Canoe. Sometimes Alice didn't want to get out of the car when they arrived at the arena until Guillaume finished his story. He was amazing. Alice loved driving with him.

"*Bonjour, ma petite!*" cried Guillaume as she opened the car door. "*Comment ça va?*"

"*Bien, merci,*" replied Alice, as Guillaume turned out of the school lot.

"Not so good out here. This freezing rain — bah! Hope you're not in a hurry. Some crazy drivers out there, eh?!"

Alice giggled. Guillaume was the craziest one of all. But even he was being careful. All around them, cars were slipping and sliding. Guillaume got stuck behind a fender bender, then made a quick turn to get around it, only to be stopped by another minor accident. Traffic ground to a halt. Guillaume turned again. Alice tightened her seatbelt, but she wasn't scared. She was with Guillaume. He eased through a back alley to get around the traffic jam. Then all the street lights went out.

"*Santa Maria!*" swore Guillaume.

"What happened?" asked Alice.

"The blackout, that's what," replied Guillaume. "All this ice, it take down a wire someplace close, kill the lights. No problem for Guillaume, but these other drivers, they know nothing. Don't know how to drive with no lights. Idiot!" Guillaume shook his fist at the driver in the next lane. Then he honked his horn. Alice raised her eyebrows. Guillaume never honked his horn. The driving must really be bad.

The streetlights flashed back on. Traffic started

moving again. Guillaume turned to his passenger.

"You sure I shouldn't take you home? No skating today?"

Alice shrugged her shoulders. "I have to go, Guillaume. My coach will be waiting." Then she grinned at him. "I'm used to ice, don't you know?!"

Guillaume cracked a smile then frowned again. "What if no lights? All close down? *Ma petite* will freeze to death on her precious ice."

But the lights were on at the arena. Guillaume took Alice right to the door. He didn't want to let her go. "Guillaume all finished for today. If the lights go out before Papa comes, you call me at home. I'll come get you. Promise?"

Alice promised. Guillaume could definitely be counted on as a friend. He waited until she was safe inside the building before he drove away.

Alice hoisted her heavy bag onto her shoulder. Now it was power skate, then freeskate, then off-ice ballet class, then solo practice.

SOPHIE COULDN'T CONCENTRATE. Her thoughts were stuck in the barn. How was Adalie doing? Was the calf born? Would it be a girl or a boy? Maybe Sébastien was right, that crazy kid. Maybe she should have told Maman how much she wanted to be with Adalie today. Sophie's feelings about the farm were getting a bit confused. Maman and Papa kept telling her that she didn't have to be a farm girl, that she could be anything she wanted to be. She wasn't sure she liked having so much choice. What was wrong with the farm? She loved every inch of it. Sophie was grateful when the bell rang.

She didn't stay grateful for long. Even though it was January and the temperature was below zero, it was still raining outside. Horrible freezing rain that hurt her face. Cold drops that froze onto her eyebrows and eyelashes. Ugh. Every year they got freezing rain at least once. Sophie was never sure why it didn't fall as snow. It had something to do with cold air and warm air smacking into each other; they'd studied it at least four times, but she couldn't remember the details. The freezing rain never lasted long, but it made life miserable. To make matters worse, the school buses were late. Probably because the freezing rain had laid an invisible coating of ice on top of everything and the snowy roads were turning into skating rinks. Sophie looked around until she found Sébastien, who was busy filming some shadow only he could see.

The school bus was an hour late. And the trip home was excruciatingly slow. Sure, the driver wanted to be careful, kids on board and all that, but why today?! Sophie was on pins and needles with worry about Adalie. As soon as the doors opened at the end of their lane, Sophie flew down the steps, only to slip on the ice and fall flat on her *derrière*. The kids on the bus exploded with laughter. How mortifying. Sophie reached her hand out to Sébastien, who was just standing there staring at her.

He pulled her up. "Can you do it again so I can film it?" he said with an absolutely straight face. As usual, Sophie couldn't tell if he was being serious or cracking a joke. She just glowered at him, and stomped up the slippery lane. Sébastien headed towards the warm glow that was the kitchen. Sophie went straight to the maternity pen.

Adalie mooed gently when Sophie came close. At her feet was the most beautiful calf Sophie had ever seen. Already standing on wobbly legs, the little heifer had enormous brown eyes and unbelievably long eyelashes. A broad smile stretched across Sophie's face, one that turned into a giggle as the calf's front legs slowly slid out from under her as if she were on ice skates. The calf looked surprised to find her chin resting on the ground and her four legs sticking out all around her like a starfish. She struggled to stand up again.

"She's strong," smiled Papa. "And determined!"

"Does she have a name?" Sophie asked, stroking the calf's soft nose.

"I was waiting for you," replied Papa.

"Mélisande," breathed Sophie. "It means strong and independent; I looked it up."

"Mélisande it is," agreed Papa. "She's nursing well and ready for her second feed of colostrum.

Interested?" Papa smiled his slow smile. Sophie didn't even need to answer, just reached for the bottle of special milk that Papa had ready. "Colostrum" was the name for the milk a mother cow gave right after the birth of a calf. It was full of special nutrients that were important for baby calves to grow and stay healthy, so all farmers made sure that newborn calves got enough of it. Papa made a note in his book. "M-é-L-I-S-A-N-D-E," he murmured to himself as he created an entry for the newest member of their herd.

When the bottle was empty, Sophie and Papa left Adalie and Mélisande together in the maternity pen. Adalie would soon have to go back to the regular barn and Mélisande into a special calf pen, but for now mother and daughter could stay together. After the warmth created by the cows in the pen, the weather outside felt truly ferocious. Not only was the icy rain still falling, but a nasty wind had blown up too. Stinging pellets burned Sophie's face as she and Papa hurried to the kitchen. They were both soaked by the time they got there.

"Baths, both of you! You first, Sophie," commanded Maman. "Only way to get you warm — *marchez!*" She marched.

ALICE WAS WORRIED. Dad was never late. But it was pretty easy to guess why. The lights in the arena had flashed off several times during practice. She could hear sirens all over the place, which meant the driving was even worse. Either Dad was stuck in traffic or he had been kept late by the power company to repair downed power lines. Their rule was that if he was delayed she had to first try to reach him by cell phone. That was usually pretty hard, as he might be up at the top of a power pole. So Alice was supposed to leave a message, then wait no more than an hour. After an hour she had to call the taxi company to take her home and leave another message to tell him where she'd gone. Almost an hour had gone by, but tonight Mr. Osborne stayed with her. He was worried.

"If your dad doesn't come soon, you're coming home with me," he told her. "This storm has a bad feel. I don't want you alone in your house."

"It's okay, Mr. O," said Alice earnestly. "I'm not afraid to be by myself."

"Well, I can wait a few more minutes," said Mr. Osborne.

And a few more minutes was all it took before Alice saw her dad inch his way into the icy parking lot. He shook hands with Mr. Osborne.

"Thanks for staying," said Dad.

"No problem," smiled Mr. Osborne. "We've got to keep our Princess safe, don't we?" Alice gave him a smile, but inwardly rolled her eyes at the nickname. *Alice, the oh-so-famous Ice Princess.* "I've cancelled tomorrow morning's practice. Even if it stops raining, the roads will be icy. By afternoon, the world should have melted."

"I was going to suggest the same thing," said Dad. "Power is out all over the place. A lot of alarm clocks won't ring tomorrow." The two men laughed.

Alice climbed into the car and soaked up the delicious heat coming from the seat. She stayed quiet so Dad could concentrate on his driving. He was nearly as good as Guillaume, if not so fast, so they made it home safe and sound.

Alice dropped her bag in the mudroom and turned to her dad.

"What do you want for dinner, Dad?"

"I'm sorry, Princess, but I have to leave. Like I said to Mr. O, power is down all over the city. The ice is starting to accumulate on the wires and it's getting really heavy. A lot of folks are going to get pretty cold tonight if we can't get the lines back up. The power company needs everybody, and we might have to work through the night. Will you be all right?"

"Oh, Dad," sighed Alice. "Do you have to?"

"I have to. You don't want people to freeze to death, do you?" *As if that was going to happen,* thought Alice. *It's just a little freezing rain.*

Dad gave her a quick hug, then bustled about getting his foul weather gear ready for a long, cold night outside. Alice turned on the coffeemaker to brew some coffee for his thermos, and while she waited, switched on the television.

Hydro-Québec is reporting limited power outages throughout the city of Montréal as a result of today's freezing rain. Broken trees and branches have fallen on power lines, bringing them to the ground and causing blackouts. Hydro crews will work through the night. Power should be restored to all areas by morning. The rain is expected to stop by noon tomorrow.

Alice sighed again, then filled Dad's thermos.

At the door, Dad stopped. "Maybe you should go stay with one of the neighbours. Maybe Mrs. Hartley next door?" he said in a worried tone. "I don't like leaving you here alone."

"No!" Alice practically shouted. *Not Mrs. Hartley!* "I'll be fine, Dad. You've left me lots of times. I'll put my cell phone by my bed in case you call. And I'll go to Mrs. Hartley's if things get really bad. I promise." Alice crossed her fingers behind her back so she wouldn't have to keep that promise. She absolutely would not go to Mrs. Hartley's for any reason, but no need for Dad to worry.

"That's my beautiful Princess," smiled Dad. He gave her a hug and went out into the storm. Alice stood on the porch to wave goodbye. He'd probably be home in a couple of hours. Then she went back inside to begin the Alone Routine. After Mom died, Dad had looked for a regular babysitter, but Alice was at the rink so much they couldn't find anybody willing to work her complicated schedule. So that's when Dad got her a cell phone and taught her the Alone Routine:

Lock front and back door

Check that garage door is down

Check that all windows are shut and locked (in summer, check screens)

Put cell phone in pocket (cell phone only to be used in emergencies to talk to Dad, all other calls on regular phone or ALICE PAYS BILL!!)

Put flashlight on kitchen table

Alice had added a few of her own ideas to Dad's routine.

Check in every cupboard and under every bed for bad or scary things

Turn all lights on in basement

Microwave a bag of popcorn

Call Sophie

Dad had found out about the long distance calls to Sophie because they were listed on the telephone bill. He didn't get mad. Instead he got a long distance phone plan and said she could call Soph whenever she wanted as long as the calls weren't on her cell phone. Dad was pretty cool.

Alice did everything on the list, put the popcorn in the microwave, then pulled the phone out to call Sophie. But she didn't punch in a single number.

Instead, Alice burst into tears.

The competition was so close. She was going to blow it – again. Alice ran upstairs to her bedroom and threw herself on her bed. Clutching Juniper, her ratty old green teddy, she cried into his plush fur until he was soaked. Then she threw him across the room. That made her stop crying. It wasn't Juniper's fault her nerves were making her feel like throwing up. She got up from the bed and picked up the soggy bear.

The popcorn was still in the microwave. It was cold. Alice punched in Sophie's number.

"Allo?"

"Bon soir, Tante Evie. May I please speak to Sophie?"

"What's wrong?" demanded her aunt.

"What do you mean?" spluttered Alice. "Nothing's wrong!"

"You've been crying, *ma petite.* Where's your dad?"

"He's at work," replied Alice, a little sullenly. She wanted to talk to Sophie, not her aunt.

"That's it, then," said Aunt Evie firmly. "You're lonely. I'll get Sophie." Alice heaved a sigh of relief. Sometimes Aunt Evie could get her to talk about stuff she didn't want to talk about. Like how she hated competing. Nobody but Sophie could know that.

"Alice, the calf is born and she's beautiful! I named her Mélisande and I've already fed her with a bottle!" Sophie's words came out in a rush. Alice had forgotten about the calf.

"Tell me about her," said Alice, in a weary voice.

"No. Not until you tell me what's wrong."

"Same old, same old, Soph. You know. I can't stop thinking about the competition when I'm alone. And because of the stupid storm, Dad has to go fix the power lines. And to make matters worse, he nearly made me go to the Tickle Lady's house!"

"Why don't you like Mrs. Hartley?" asked Sophie curiously.

"Because she...well, she's really..." Alice hesitated. "Because nobody likes her," she finally said tentatively.

"But why?" persisted Sophie.

Alice sighed. "The kids in the neighbourhood used to play shinny in the street. She always yelled at them for making too much noise. Then one day this kid really roofed it, the ball went over the net and through her window. She came running out like a crazy lady. The kids went nuts, 'cause it turns out she has these incredibly long fingernails, like four inches or something. She chased after the kids waving these claws in the air, and the story got out that if she caught you she would take you inside her house and tickle you until her nails scratched you to death." When spoken aloud, the story sounded lame even to Alice.

Sophie burst out laughing. "That means you should go over there and see if it's true. Then you can tell everybody that you are *très courageuse* and they will make you their hero!"

"It doesn't matter," said Alice quietly. "I don't have time to play shinny. I don't even see the kids on the street any more. Sophie, tell me everything about Mélisande. Don't leave anything out."

The two girls settled in for a long talk. Neither noticed that the wind outside had picked up and the freezing rain was falling even harder.

DAY TWO
Tuesday, January 6, 1998

SLEEPILY, ALICE REACHED OVER TO PUSH THE OFF button of her alarm. How she hated that thing. It kept buzzing and buzzing. She rolled over, still with her eyes shut, and pushed the button a second time. The buzzing still wouldn't stop. Alice opened her eyes. It wasn't the alarm. It was her phone. She grabbed the cell from her bedside table.

"Daddy?" she asked.

"It's me, Princess," Dad replied. "How are you doing?"

Alice's brain was starting to wake up. There was light coming through her window; it was morning already. That felt weird. She always got up in the dark. "What time is it?"

"It's 7:30, sleepyhead. Practice is cancelled this morning, remember?"

"Oh, yeah." Alice felt groggy from sleeping in.

"And it's not the only thing that's cancelled," Dad went on. "School is closed as well. Montréal is a mess. Power lines are busted all over the place and there are lots of people with no electricity. The police want everybody to stay home until this blasted freezing rain stops."

Alice switched on her bedside lamp. Nothing happened. "Daddy, our power is off too! Last night the television said it would be all over by this morning."

"I know. It's a little worse than we first thought. Look, here's the plan. I'm going to work a few more hours, then I'm coming home for a bit of a sleep. After that I have to go back to work. I want you to get warm clothes on and stay put. Try not to open the refrigerator door too often, because we want the food to keep cold as long as possible. Did you put the flashlight on the kitchen table last night?"

"Yup," Alice nodded into the phone.

"Good. There are some candles in the bottom kitchen drawer. Get them, some saucers and the matches. Melt the bottom of the candles a bit with the match flame, just enough so you can stick them up on the saucers so they won't tip and start a fire if we have to light them. Next, go around the house and unplug everything you can think of – the TV, the computer, the coffee maker and the clocks. Then look in my top dresser drawer."

"In your bedroom?" asked Alice.

"Yes. There's an old-fashioned radio in there with a little windup handle. This is important, Princess. If you wind the handle, it powers up the radio. No electricity needed. You can tune it to a local station to hear what's going on around town, even if the TV or the regular radio doesn't work. Thank goodness for the good old days, eh?!" Alice rolled her eyes.

"I'll be home in a few hours. Power will probably be back by this afternoon, but it's good practice to be prepared. Make sure you don't leave the house, Alice, unless it's to go to Mrs. Hartley's. Things are a little crazy right now, so that's the most important thing."

"Okay, Dad," promised Alice. No need for crossed fingers for this promise. There was nowhere she wanted to go.

"One more thing. The phone lines might come down. The telephone companies have generators just in case, but they might not have enough of them, so our home phone might not work. We can use our cells for a while, but when the batteries go we won't be able to recharge. I just don't want you to be scared if you don't hear from me. I'm all right; it just means I'm not close to a working phone. Okay? I love you, Princess."

"I love you too, Daddy," said Alice. She hung up the phone, feeling a little bewildered. Dad was making the situation sound serious, but they'd had blackouts lots of times. They weren't such a big deal, especially in the daytime. Oh well. Alice cuddled back down under her warm blanket. Her room felt cold, colder than usual. There was no rush to get out of her cozy bed. All she had to do was get the candles and the radio and then she'd... It was kind of hard to think of what she might do. No skating, no school. She wasn't used to having nowhere to go and nothing to do.

MAMAN TOLD SOPHIE AND SÉBASTIEN at breakfast that the school buses were still running, but after waiting nearly forty minutes at the end of the lane Sophie gave up.

"I'm going back to the house," she said to Sébastien. "I hate this rain. Wait if you want. I'm too cold."

The kitchen was way cozier than the end of the lane. Maman was baking, the wood stove was sending out waves of heat and the radio was playing one of Maman's soft rock favourites. That made Sophie smile to herself. Maman's version of rock and roll was so old fashioned! But she was old, way over thirty, so that was to be expected, Sophie guessed. She pulled off her down jacket and mitts and plopped down on a kitchen chair near the stove.

"No school for us today," grinned Sophie. "Guess I'll have to help Papa in the barn!"

"No school, my foot," laughed Maman. "No bus is

not the same as no school, *ma petite*. Get dressed again while I start the truck. I'll take you in."

Sophie groaned, but did as she was told. She waited in the kitchen for the truck to warm up enough to melt the ice on the windshield. Great columns of hot fumes from the exhaust pipe swirled around it, melting the pellets of ice into real rain. This, thought Sophie, was officially really icky weather. She was about to walk out to the truck when the phone rang.

"Hey, Soph, it's Alice. Cool to have no school, eh?"

"Lucky you," replied Sophie. "We have to go. Sébastien and I have been waiting for the bus for, like, hours, and now Maman is going to drive us."

"Wow," said Alice. "The ice must not be so bad in Saint-Hyacinthe, then. Dad says Montréal is practically shut down. Power's out, phones might go out, practically everything's closed." Alice couldn't help exaggerating a little. It was exciting to be the princess in distress, even if it was just a little distress, a fairly comfortable distress.

"Dad's got me getting candles out, managing the radio communications, stuff like that. I mean, there's no one else to do it, 'cause he has to work." Alice felt strong, coping all by herself. She grinned and stood a little taller even though Sophie couldn't see her.

"Yeah, yeah, yeah," teased Sophie. "You city folk have it so rough! You get a little ice and the whole city shuts down. Make sure you don't burn the house down with your candles!"

"All right, all right," laughed Alice. "So it's not so bad. But I still get a day off school, so there!"

Sophie had to hang up. The truck was ready to roll. She ran outside and hopped into the front seat. Sébastien was still valiantly waiting for the school bus at the end of the lane. Sophie made him crawl behind her into the back seat when they picked him up. Maman turned carefully onto the concession road that led to the school. It was sheer ice.

"Maybe this wasn't such a good idea," she murmured. "The ice is worse than I thought."

"But, Maman, I have a test today," said Sébastien. "It's very important!" Sophie scowled. Most kids would be glad for an excuse to miss a test, but not *her* brother.

"*Oui, oui, mon fils,* I shall get you to school. But *mon Dieu,* this is awful!"

Classes at the school were only half full. A lot of kids couldn't get in. Sébastien's test was cancelled. Sophie loved weather days at school. They got to play Seven Up in class and watch movies and fool around in the gym because none of the teachers wanted the absent students to miss out on anything important. As far as Sophie was concerned, it could keep on raining. All play and no work at school with her friends made for a perfect day as far as she was concerned.

ALICE SAT ON THE COUCH IN THE LIVING ROOM for a while, staring at the wall, then she wandered into the dining room. She peered through the sliding doors. The backyard was beautiful. The snow was perfect with not a single footprint to mess it up. Everything she could see looked like it was made of glass. If she stepped out there, Alice wondered, would the whole glittery world shatter into a million pieces, showing the ordinary world beneath?

There was a huge forked maple tree near the fence that separated their backyard from Mrs. Hartley's. Every branch had its very own ice blanket, making the tree shine white against the gloomy grey sky. It was like the world a snow queen should live in. Or maybe an Ice Princess, like her. Cold and stark and beautiful with a protective coating that nobody could break through. Alice frowned and went back to the living room. Even school would be more fun than sitting here all alone. Thinking.

Worrying made Alice feel agitated. She couldn't sit still, so she tried running on the spot and doing jumping jacks. That was lame. She decided to sing at the top of her lungs. The only song she could remember was one she'd heard on Guillaume's car radio. She was a lousy singer. And it was a stupid song.

She didn't feel like reading. She couldn't run the washing machine. She couldn't microwave a snack.

She couldn't watch TV. Besides Soph, she really didn't have anybody else to call. She wished her computer was a laptop. Then she'd have something to do, at least until the batteries ran out. Alice sighed. Weather days didn't come very often, so they should be fun. This was just boring. Finally, Alice got an old deck of cards from the kitchen drawer and started building a house of cards. How exciting was that? Then she remembered the radio.

Alice sat down on a kitchen chair and looked it over. The crank pulled out from the side. It was hard to turn at first, really sticky, but with a little elbow grease she got it turning. How long did you have to crank it? Alice gave it a good twenty turns, then pushed the on button. Nothing. She gave it another twenty and got static. She turned the dial. Some stations were clearer than others, but she still couldn't make out the words. Ah – she needed an aerial. The radio must have been built in the Dark Ages. What kind of radio needed an aerial these days? Alice found the long silver piece on the other side of the radio and extended it full out. Turning the dial again, her favourite station came in loud and clear.

Tens of thousands of people in Montreal are still without power this morning. Hospital emergency rooms are jammed with people suffering from hip, leg and arm fractures due to slips and falls on icy side-

walks. Getting around the city is difficult, with some roads closed for ice removal. Police are asking Montréalers to stay home if at all possible until crews get ahead of the ice. Old-timers suggest that this may be our worst storm in four decades.

Alice shivered. She couldn't tell if it was the bad news, or the cold. Because it *was* cold. Alice frowned and checked the thermostat on the living room wall. The house was down to sixteen degrees. They usually kept it at twenty or twenty-one in the winter. No wonder she was shivering.

The phone rang. Alice jumped up.

"Dad?!" she cried.

"No, *ma petite, c'est* Uncle Henri. Sophie, she says you are in the dark and your dad is away. Are you all right?"

Alice sat down. "Sure, Uncle Henri, I'm just fine. Dad gave me instructions and I did everything he said. He'll be home soon. I'm staying put, just like he told me."

"*C'est bon.* Did you open the pipes?" asked Uncle Henri.

"What?" asked Alice. "I don't know what you mean."

"If your house gets too cold, the water in your pipes might freeze and the pipes will crack. It will be a big problem for you. Better to open them up, keep the water running."

"But Uncle Henri, the power will be back on soon. Won't they be okay?"

"Peut-être, but better to be prepared. Go upstairs to your bathroom and turn on the taps. Just a little, so there is a steady drip, drip, drip. Running water is not so likely to freeze. *D'accord?"*

"Okay, if you say so, Uncle Henri," Alice replied.

"Bien," said Uncle Henri firmly. "Tell your Papa to call me when he gets home. Maybe you should come here. We have no power problems like the city. Then your Papa won't worry about you."

"I'll tell him, but Uncle Henri, it's going to be fine. The power will be back on soon," Alice assured him.

"Peut-être," replied her uncle. "But, *ma petite,* just in case, you call us if you need us. Promise?"

"I promise," said Alice before she hung up. So many promises. Why were all the grown-ups so worried?

UNCLE HENRI PUT DOWN THE PHONE thoughtfully. Alice, she was a tough nut. Evie was sure she'd been crying earlier, which meant his niece was either scared of the storm or lonely for company or both. But Alice would never admit to feelings of weakness. Even when it was obvious that she was in the midst of a disaster – Henri shook his head as he recalled some of Alice's more spectacular competition disasters – she always pretended that everything was all right. But was it?

This storm was going to be a monster, Henri could feel it. The clouds above had settled in to stay. His farmer's instinct told him that the rain wasn't going away. The ice was going to continue to build up on the power lines, on the trees, on the houses and the roads. His family would be fine at the farm. They had a wood stove and a power generator. But the city folks depended on being able to plug their lives in all the time. Life was going to get tough in Montréal. Tough for his *petite* Alice. Henri glanced over at Sophie and Sébastien arguing as usual over some kind of video game. He smiled. Yes, Alice needed to be with them. He'd drive over the bridge to the city first thing in the morning and collect her, so she'd be safe. So she wouldn't have to pretend to be so strong all the time, *pauvre petite.*

ALICE TRIED TO BE PATIENT. She'd turned on the bathroom and the kitchen taps just a little like Uncle Henri told her, but the drip, drip, drip was driving her nuts. She decided to call Sophie. Tried to, anyway, but there was no dial tone. Just like Dad had said, the phone lines had come down too. Would Dad get mad if she tried her cell? Probably not; she didn't have a choice, right? Unfortunately, her cell was dead. Stupid – why hadn't she remembered to charge it last night when they had power?

Alice tried to read. She really liked to read. It was something she could do in between practices at the rink and something that made her look busy at school when all the other kids were hanging out and didn't bother to include her. But Alice couldn't concentrate on the story. Now that she had all the time in the world, hours and hours to read if she wanted, she didn't feel like it any more.

The house was getting really cold. The day hadn't been that bad, just a little below zero, but the temperature in the house had dropped to twelve degrees. Which wasn't horrible, Alice had to admit, but it was uncomfortable. She added another layer of sweats around dinnertime. She tried the phone for the hundredth time. Nothing. She looked out the window. It was dark and she couldn't see anything. She took the candle to the living room and pulled out one of the old photo albums. Turning the pages slowly, she wondered when she'd last looked at the pictures. Alice at three, wobbly on her skates, wearing a pink angora sweater and a white knit skirt. Alice at six, in sequins now, holding her first trophy. Alice and Mom in the basement, Mom's mouth full of pins and Alice making a funny face as Mom fitted a new skating costume on her. That made Alice sad. Now she remembered why she didn't look at the albums any more. She wandered into the kitchen, looking longingly at the microwave popcorn box. She held up the candle and peered into the pantry. Were there any M&Ms left? Maybe she could sort them into colours. Oh, she was *so* bored.

Where was her dad? It had been dark for ages and he still wasn't home.

Just when she felt like she was going to scream in frustration, Dad's headlights came up the drive. Alice jumped up.

"How's my Princess?" called Dad, as he took off his foul weather gear in the mudroom.

"Daddy! You're home!"

"And thank goodness for that, is all I can say," replied Dad. "I'm exhausted."

Alice looked at her dad critically. He did look awfully tired. Before Mom died, she asked Alice to look after Dad. Alice took that responsibility very seriously. After all, he looked after her. There had to be somebody who looked after him.

"Daddy, you should have a warm bath while I make you some coffee," said Alice with a worried frown.

"I would love that, Princess," smiled her Dad. "But no hot water and no coffee maker. How about dry clothes, a blanket, and hot chocolate on the barbecue?"

Alice groaned. "I forgot. I can get the blanket but I don't know how to make hot chocolate on the barbecue."

"Me neither," said Dad with a tired grin. "I guess we'll have to find out."

Dad looked a little better once he'd changed into dry,

warm clothes. "I noticed the bathroom taps were dripping – that was smart thinking. Good girl!" said Dad.

"It was Uncle Henri's idea. He called. He wants you to call him. Does your cell still have power? He thinks I should go to the farm. I mean, Dad, that'd be cool but the power will be back on soon and I'd miss practice!"

Dad sighed. "It's not so easy, Princess. This storm is worse than we thought, and the weatherman says it's not going to stop raining today. Power might be out for a while. And no, my cell is dead until I can find someplace to recharge it. But that's not going to happen anytime soon, since I only get sent to places with no power."

Alice frowned. "How long before everything's fixed?"

Dad shook his head wearily. "The only thing I know is that I have to be back to work in six hours. I need to eat, then I'm going to bed."

Dinner was hot chocolate and whatever was in the freezer that was likely to go bad first if the power stayed off. Pork chops, frozen fries, frozen peas and *lots* of ice cream. Not that ice cream was very appealing when they were both freezing already, but Alice couldn't bear to throw out Bernett's chocolate raspberry truffle. Dad froze himself all over again standing on the deck doing the barbecuing. But the hot food tasted good.

Alice had had the whole day to plan the evening with her dad. "Dad, do you want to play cribbage? After that, I've got out the old Scrabble game and we can play by candlelight."

"That sounds great. But your old dad has to be up very soon. If I'm not, it'll be another dinner on the barbecue and you don't want that!" Dad tried to joke but Alice could see how tired he was. She wasn't sure he'd actually make it to his bed before he fell asleep. She kissed him good night, and then went to the kitchen to clean the dishes as best she could with cold water.

The crank radio was sitting on the kitchen table. Alice eyed it warily. She wasn't sure she wanted any more news, since it all seemed to be bad.

All of a sudden the phone rang. Yahoo! The phones were working! Could the power be far behind? Alice grabbed the receiver.

"Hello?"

"Bon soir, ma petite," Uncle Henri's deep voice came across the line. *"Comment ça va?"*

"Daddy's home, Uncle Henri," replied Alice. "We're okay. But Dad's really tired; he's sleeping. Our phones weren't working before. Want me to wake him up?"

"Non, your Papa has a big job to do. Let him sleep. I call to say I come tomorrow to get you and bring you to the farm. Tell your Papa. Even if we lose

power too, we have the wood stove and the generator. Tell your Papa we will look after you so he doesn't have to worry."

Alice grinned. "That'll be great Uncle Henri! When should I be ready?"

"After lunch, *ma petite*. The roads are very bad. It will take a while to get to your house, even with the four-wheel drive."

"Okay. I'll be packed," said Alice. "Uncle Henri? Um, thanks."

Alice hung up the phone. She was going to Sophie's! If this was going to last a while like Dad said and the radio said, it would be way more fun at the farm than sitting around home all by herself. Alice ran to the doorway of her dad's bedroom to see if he was awake. She wanted to tell him right away. But he was asleep. Alice sighed. She'd tell him tomorrow. He'd be glad; she knew he would.

Alice was too excited to sleep. Once more she tried to read, and this time she was able to relax into the story. Probably because Dad was home and everything was okay now. She read chapter after chapter but finally had to stop. Reading by candlelight made her eyes sore. What else was there to do all by herself? She lay back on the couch. The candles made odd shadows.

Raising her hands, Alice put two fingers in front of the flame. Her hands made the shape of a bunny on the wall. Smiling, she tried another shape, moving her fingers back and forth. There, that one was a bulldog! She sat up. If she used her whole arm she could make a goose. Two hands made a tortoise. Eight fingers made a flying bird. This was fun! Alice tried shadow after shadow until the candle burned down to almost nothing and there was truly nothing left to do except go to bed.

Alice went to the bathroom to brush her teeth. She picked up the toothpaste tube but it wouldn't squeeze. The toothpaste inside was too cold, nearly frozen. Alice shook her head. This was getting ridiculous.

DAY THREE
Wednesday, January 7, 1998

ALICE PULLED THE COVERS OVER HER HEAD. SHE reached down into the bottom of her bed for her clothes before she remembered she was already wearing them. She'd gone to bed wearing her tights, two sets of sweats and her toque. No wonder she felt like she couldn't move. Alice peeked out from under the covers. It was probably morning, but you could hardly tell. It was the kind of dark day that forced teachers to turn all the lights on in the classroom as if it was night. She pulled her toque off and listened to the wind howling outside. It sounded like someone was throwing pebbles against her window over and over again. But it wasn't pebbles. It was tiny slivers of ice. It was still raining.

Poor Dad. He'd left much earlier, Alice didn't know how early but it had still been dark. She'd stumbled out of bed to give him a hug and tell him she was going to the farm, and then gone right back to bed.

Even without getting out of bed, she knew the house was colder. That meant there was still no power. But, thought Alice, it never hurts to try. She rolled over on her stomach, snaked her arm out from under the covers and reached behind her bedside table. Feeling with her fingers, she found the plug for her reading light and plugged it in. She held her breath and flicked the switch. Nothing.

She unplugged the light then cuddled back under the covers. Alice couldn't wait until she was in Saint-Hyacinthe with Sophie. At least she'd have somebody to talk to. But Uncle Henri wasn't coming until after lunch, so Alice reached for her book and made a nest for herself under the covers. She might as well stay in bed and keep warm until it was time to go.

EVEN MAMAN HAD DECREED NO SCHOOL that morning, but she still wouldn't let Sophie go with Papa to get Alice.

"The roads are terrible," said Maman firmly.

Sophie remembered what Sébastien had said. Tell her what you really want. She'll listen.

"Maman, this is really important to me. I'm worried about Alice. And I want to see the ice on all the trees! Please, Maman?"

"*Non, ma jeune fille.* You cannot always have what you

want. This time, it is just too dangerous," replied Maman.

You can't always have what you want, grumbled Sophie to herself. How about never getting what you want? Sébastien didn't know what he was talking about.

Papa gave her a hug. "I need you to look after the animals while I'm gone, *ma chou*. The trip might take longer than usual, and you know the animals can't wait to be watered or milked. I need you – you too, Sébastien – to help your Maman."

Generally Sophie was too old to be palmed off with the "I really need your help" line. But in this case, she knew her father was right. If he didn't make it back by three o'clock, Maman would need both of them to help with the milking. They had fifty head of cattle, after all. If the milking was late, they would have to listen to fifty cows bawl for attention, and that was like something out of one of Sébastien's horror stories.

Maman filled Papa's thermos with hot chocolate and Sophie helped pack him a good lunch for the road. It was only fifty kilometres to the city and shouldn't take more than an hour, but with the ice the trip was bound to be slower. Papa scraped ice off the four-wheel drive while the motor warmed up. It was raining so hard he had to change into dry clothes when he was finished. Sophie waved him off and headed to the maternity pen to visit Adalie and Mélisande. Papa would probably move Adalie back to the main barn this afternoon, and then Sophie would be completely in charge of feeding Mélisande. Sophie loved being in charge of a calf, loved being needed like that. It felt like the most important job in the world.

ALICE'S LEGS WERE STARTING TO TWITCH under the covers. She just couldn't stay still for so long, cold or no cold. Even though she had only missed one day of practice, her muscles were starting to itch with inactivity. She got out of bed and checked her dad's bedroom, just to make sure he was gone and not sleeping. Gone. Without really wanting to, she headed next to the thermostat on the wall. The house had lost another four degrees overnight; the temperature was down to eight. Once Dad had told her that a refrigerator should be kept at three degrees Celsius. Five more degrees and she'd be living inside a fridge. She decided to put on a fleece vest over her other layers.

She wandered out to the kitchen. Alice wished her dad had taught her how to make hot chocolate on the barbecue; a hot drink would be nice. He hadn't. All he had done was tell her she *couldn't* use their camp stove in the kitchen. Alice couldn't understand why, because she knew how to work that one. He said it was dangerous to light them inside the house, but really, she wouldn't have had it on for very long. Well, it didn't matter. By evening she would be at the farm and Aunt Evie would cook one of her delicious meals on their wood stove. Dad had been really happy when she told him about Uncle Henri's call.

Alice poured herself cereal and got some milk from the fridge. She sniffed it. It didn't smell great but it wasn't sour yet. As the house got colder, the fridge got warmer. Weird. Before she picked up her spoon, she cranked up the radio. Maybe it would have good news.

At this point, millions are without power. The Montréal area is the hardest hit. Police are evacuating the elderly to shelters throughout the city. Power outages extend to Kingston in the west and New Hampshire in the east. The nation's capital is frozen solid. Ottawa is virtually closed for business. Police encourage all residents affected by the ice storm to stay off the roads. 911 calls have swamped the emergency system. Please stay off the lines except for true medical emergencies.

Alice's eyes grew large. What on earth? Millions without power? Millions? No wonder her dad had to stay at work. Dad had said the storm was worse than anybody had originally thought, but still...millions?

Alice turned off the radio. She ran to look out the sliding doors in the dining room. The back yard had changed. The ice was thicker, much thicker. She bet it would hold her now. But if Alice knew anything, she knew ice, and this stuff looked super slippery. She sure wasn't going to try it out. She looked at the big old maple tree. The tiny blankets of ice wrapped round all the branches were fat tubes now, several centimetres thick, dragging the tree down. Every branch had splayed away from the trunk. Some drooped so low that the tips were frozen right into the ground, making frozen archways. That thirty-metre tree was only about ten metres tall now.

Alice ran to the front hall. Her whole street was dead still; not a single person was moving, not a single car. She stepped outside onto the porch. The world was so quiet. No sirens, no traffic, no people talking on cell phones, no dogs barking, no kids laughing. It was so quiet she could hear the light sound of the freezing rain falling, followed by an abrupt silence as each droplet froze in place. She could hear the wind blowing tiny pellets of ice and frozen snow against the windows, making a scratchy sound. And all around her, the world groaned. The groaning seemed to come from nowhere and from everywhere. She listened harder. It was coming from the trees and the power lines and the houses. They groaned under the weight of the ice. Alice began to breathe heavily. She couldn't help it; hearing the groans made her feel as if a weight was sitting on her chest as well. She tried to slow her breathing down, tried to imagine the weight lifting. All of a sudden there was a rifle shot.

Alice's lungs exploded in a great exhale. Terrified, she jumped back into the safety of the doorway. The shot was followed by a tinkling of glass, a shower of broken bits that shattered when they hit the icy street. Finally, there was a breathy whoosh, as if something heavy had fallen onto something soft. Then there was silence.

Alice was panting, from fear this time. Had somebody died? Had some maniac shot through a window and killed somebody who fell into a snowbank? On *her* street? Alice heard shouts down the street. Cautiously she peeked around the door.

In the middle of the road was a majestic maple tree. It lay broken and twisted in a sea of shattered branches. Dead – killed by the ice as surely as if it had been shot. The two biggest branches in its crown had buckled under the weight of ice and fallen in opposite directions, splitting the trunk right down to the ground. The heart of the maple had been violently torn apart, baring its dark interior surrounded by the broken bones of fresh yellow wood. Alice had never really taken much notice of the tree but had the weird feeling that she wanted to cry.

The neighbours milled around the carcass. Where had they all come from? Had everyone been hiding inside their homes? One of them got a gas-powered chainsaw from his garage and revved it up. Alice couldn't watch them further dismember the tree so she went back inside. She could hear the whine of the chainsaw even from the kitchen and it sounded worse than fingernails on a chalkboard. She went back to bed and pulled the covers over her head. This wasn't an ordinary blackout.

Alice was well and truly scared. Uncle Henri couldn't come soon enough.

HENRI WAS HAVING A HARD TIME staying on the road. The trip had taken three times as long as normal, but he was nearly to the bridge that led to the city of Montréal. On the radio, announcers talked about damage completely beyond Henri's ability to imagine. How could two days of freezing rain do so much harm? How could so much of the power grid be down? The announcer talked about pylons being crushed by the weight of the ice, twisted and flattened into useless metal sculptures. Surely that was impossible. Pylons were transmission towers made of tonnes of steel, some reaching 175 metres into the sky. How much ice would it take to crush such a structure? Henri could only shake his head. The radio once more caught his attention.

Breaking news: The major power substation in Saint-Hyacinthe has just failed.

Henri had to concentrate hard not to slip off the road. So, they had lost their power too. It wasn't an immediate problem for his family as they had a generator to use for backup power. But lots of his neighbours didn't have one. Generators, at least the size you needed to run a dairy farm, were very expensive, thousands of dollars for something you might never need. But his neighbours did have cows. Cows that needed to be watered and milked, tasks that required power. Lots of it. He needed to get home.

But what of *petite* Alice? All alone in the dark? He had promised to get her. Henri was torn. She was a good girl and her dad would be checking in as often as possible. Could she be brave? Or would she be better off at the farm? Probably. At least no one would have to worry about her there. He'd come so far, after all.

Attention: We have just been informed that bridges to the island of Montréal are closing. Ice buildup has reached the point that there is a grave danger of injury and death from ice falling from the overhead structures of the bridges. We repeat: bridges to the island of Montréal are closed.

The decision was made for him. There was no way to get to Alice that didn't involve a bridge. She would *have* to be brave. Henri said a quick prayer for her and turned the four-wheel drive around.

SOPHIE HATED PLAYING VIDEO GAMES with Sébastien. The games he liked were all about strategy, and Sébastien's mind worked in such devious ways that it was like playing with a crazy person. Sophie had had to learn to be a good loser because winning was an impossible feat around her brother. And she didn't like it – not one bit. Who likes to lose all the time? Sophie could think one, maybe two moves in advance. She generally expected her opponent to make the same moves she would, but Sébastien never did. And yet the ridiculous things he did always worked in the end, leaving her trapped with no power, no weapons, no spare lives and no way out. Sophie truly couldn't understand how he did it, and it made her feel so frustrated. But she played anyway; she didn't know why. Maybe because Sébastien seemed to like it so much.

When the power failed and the screen went dark, Sophie was, of course, losing. "All right, oh great master," she conceded grudgingly. "You win already. Get your coat on. We'll have to help Maman get the generator out. Milking starts in an hour." Sébastien grumbled too, but did as he was told. Sophie was secretly relieved. Maman wouldn't let them play video games on generator power; she'd say it was a waste. So Sophie wouldn't have to endure any more humiliation for a while. They were about to leave for the barn when the phone rang. Good thing the phones hadn't gone when the power did.

"*Allo, bonjour,*" said Sophie.

It was their neighbour down the road. Could they borrow the generator? Sophie said she'd have Maman call them, and hung up. The phone rang again.

"*Allo, bonjour,*" said Sophie again.

Another neighbour. Another request for the generator. Sophie gave the same answer, and hung up. The phone rang a third time. Sophie just looked at it. She decided to let it ring. Better for Maman to talk to their neighbours. She would know how many farms they could squeeze onto their generator.

Out in the shed, Maman had already hooked the tractor up to the generator. "Drive it out to the pole, will you Sophie?" Maman called out. Sophie hopped up onto the tractor. Slowly and carefully she eased the heavy load out into the rain and inched down the drive. Boy, was it slippery! She hadn't been driving the tractor for very long, and she'd never driven it on ice. She crept along until she reached the hydro pole that had the special generator panel box on it. Once the generator was hooked up, all they had to do was flick a switch and the generator would send power to the house, the barn and the water pump. Her parents had complained about the cost of the special switch but decided to get it anyway, reasoning that the time they needed the generator would be the time they would kick themselves if they hadn't installed the switch too.

While Sophie crept down the drive, Maman went back to the house to put on more clothes. Hooking up the generator wasn't the easiest thing in the world. It took the two of them nearly a half-hour in the freezing rain to get it done. But when Maman flicked the switch, it was all worth it. Lights came on in the house and the fans starting whirring in the barn. With a grin, Sophie high-fived Maman.

"Maman, Monsieur Boisvert and Madame de Bellefeuille called. They want to use the generator. I said you'd call them back. The phone kept ringing, but I didn't pick it up. How many people can we share with?" asked Sophie.

Maman sighed. "Not as many as will need it," she replied. "The chores will take longer because the generator can only put out 50 kW of power. We can't run all the machines at once. Let's see how long it takes to do our milking and then I'll know how much generator time we can loan out. Sébastien!" she called. "Get the first lot moving into the milking parlour and then fill the water trough as high as you can. Sophie and I will start to hook them up."

While Sébastien started the electric pump to bring water from the well to the cows, Sophie and Maman started working with the first ten cows. They had what was called a herringbone milking parlour – a long thin barn with a pit up the middle and a row of five milking stalls on either side. The milking stalls were on an angle, which is why it was called a herringbone. It did kind of look like a fish bone: the pit was the spine and the stalls were the ribs. The cows' heads faced away from the middle so that their udders were close to the pit, where the farmers worked. Why it was called a parlour, Sophie had no idea. Maybe because they worked so hard to make their cows comfortable that it was almost nicer than their living room?

THE FIRST TEN COWS MEANDERED INTO THE milking parlour. They angled off, five to each side, one to a stall. They knew what to do. Sophie and Maman went down into the pit. It was like a hallway that was partly below ground. It made the cows' udders easy to reach. It had white, tiled walls that were easy to clean, and the floor was concrete, with a good rubber mat on top. Once the stalls were full, Maman took one side and Sophie the other. They each took a hose and cleaned all the mud and dirt off the cows' udders and back legs. Before they touched the cows, they snapped on plastic gloves like a doctor and went along the row, dipping each cow's four teats into a teat cup to clean them. Next the teats were gently dried with a soft, disposable cloth, a fresh cloth for every cow. Sophie always gave each cow a little pat on the side when she was drying her. It was a good chance to say hello and check that the cow was nice and calm and feeling well. Each one was like a member of the family. They always milked better when they were happy. Finally, Sophie and Maman attached the electronic milking machines to each cow's teats. Gentle suction massaged the teats, creating great rivers of milk that began to flow through the tubes into the receiving jars. Maman stared at the filling tank with a worried look on her face.

"What's wrong?" asked Sophie.

"When we loan out the generator, we won't be able to keep the cooler running. The milk will spoil."

"Maybe we shouldn't loan it, then," replied Sophie. "I mean, not if we need it."

"Ever hear the expression, *don't cry over spilt milk?*" said Maman gently. "It will be a shame to lose the milk, but that's nothing compared to the pain the cows on those other farms will feel if we don't share the generator. If they don't get milked, they could get an awful infection. If the fans don't keep the air fresh in the barns, they could get pneumonia. If they don't get watered, they could die."

Sophie frowned as she watched the milking machines automatically drop off each cow when the milking was done. She moved along the pit, gently dipping each teat into a soothing mix of lanolin and iodine for a final clean. Then she pushed the release button on the milking stall gates, letting the cows out to make room for the next group. She was thoughtful.

What if they didn't have a generator? Could Adalie and Mélisande die?

Sophie hung her head. She was ashamed. "I'm sorry, Maman. I didn't think."

Maman gave her a quick squeeze. "I know you didn't mean to be selfish. When things go wrong, it's hard to think. Everything that you know changes and you have to change with it, and you have to do it fast, before there really is any time to think. It's easy to make mistakes."

"But you know what to do!" exclaimed Sophie. "You didn't forget anything."

"That's because Papa and I planned for this. Remember two years ago when we had to give up our trip to Disney World? And you and Sébastien were so disappointed? We were disappointed too, but we were worried about our cows. About what would happen to them if we lost power. So we spent the money on the generator instead of the trip." Maman smiled. "It's much easier thinking about what to do before the disaster than when you're in it!"

Maman was right. Today, a generator was definitely way more exciting than Disney World. Sophie smiled. She never thought she'd think something like that!

ALICE WAS READING IN BED when Dad came home. She jumped up and ran to the mud room to meet him. He looked so tired and cold! He came into the kitchen, sat heavily on a chair, and put his head in his hands.

"I don't have long," he said wearily. "Just time for a short nap. I was hoping to find you gone, safe with Uncle Henri. Have you heard from him yet?"

Alice shook her head. "He said he'd come some-time after lunch."

"I'll try the phone. Maybe Evie knows where he is." Dad picked up the receiver and frowned. "Phones are gone again," he said with a sigh. "Disasters some-times bring out the absolute worst in people, that's for sure." He shook his head sadly.

"What do you mean?" asked Alice curiously.

"The telephone companies have their own genera-tors. When the phones lose power, they can restore it by hooking the phone lines to the generators. But there are people out there who are wandering around with pickup trucks, stealing every generator they can find so they can sell them for a profit. They don't care how much that hurts people who can't phone for help."

Alice was shocked, and disgusted. "People really do that?"

"They really do, Princess, they really do. Listen, I'll show you how to use the barbecue while I'm here. Just in case Uncle Henri gets held up. I don't know when I'll be back to the house again. Our crew is moving outside the city to work on one of the major lines that feed electricity into Montréal. I may be sleeping in a tent tonight."

"A tree fell down right in the middle of the street," said Alice, "because of the ice. Is that what's happening to the power lines?"

"That's exactly what's happening," replied Dad, as he got up to start the barbecue. "The lines are able to with-stand a certain amount of ice, but not this much. Worse than that, the transmission towers that link the lines together are collapsing. They can withstand 45 mm of ice – that's almost two inches. But some places have 100 mm of ice. That's more than four inches – twice as much as they can handle. The towers will take weeks to repair." Dad sighed. "I've never seen anything like it."

Alice filled a pot with water that Dad could boil on the barbecue. She watched carefully as he taught her how to regulate the gas, and how to be safe when she lit the flame. He checked the freezer. The food inside was starting to thaw.

"Only use stuff that feels like it's still a little frozen, just in case," said Dad. "After that, heat up stuff in tins or boxes. Do we have any canned spaghetti?"

There was some chicken that still felt a bit frozen, so they didn't need to resort to tinned spaghetti yet. While Dad took a nap, Alice boiled more water to keep in a thermos for later. Within an hour, Dad was back on the move.

"Are you sure you're okay?" he asked, as he gave her a tight hug. "I hate to leave you like this."

"I'm fine, Dad," Alice assured him. "Don't worry about me. Uncle Henri will probably come just after you leave and then I'll be safe at the farm. You just worry about the transmission towers. Now that I can use the barbecue, I can make hot food if he's late. Just be careful, okay?"

Then he was gone. Alice stood at the door until his big hydro truck had inched its way down the street and turned the corner. She didn't really feel okay at all.

Dad's wasn't the only vehicle inching down the street. It looked like a lot of her neighbours were packing up and leaving. Maybe the tree had scared them too. She waved at a couple of them as they went by. The Thibeau family stopped at her curb and Madame Thibeau rolled the car window down.

"Alice," she shouted. "Is your father working?"

"Yes, he is," Alice called back.

"We're going to a hotel that still has power. Come with us. You can leave a note for your dad." Madame Thibeau smiled. "The hotel has a pool!"

Alice grinned back. "Thanks, but my uncle is coming to get me. I'm going to stay with my cousins."

"C'est bon. Stay warm!" She waved and rolled up the window as her husband eased the car forward. *Well,* thought Alice. *That was cool of them. At least some people are still nice.*

Alice went inside and tried the phone again. There was no dial tone. Where was Uncle Henri? It was way past lunch. Alice checked that the backpack she had filled with her overnight stuff was ready at the front door and picked up her book.

Two hours later, the already dark and gloomy sky started to get darker. Alice finally admitted to herself that Uncle Henri wasn't coming. At least not today. Something must have happened. Even thinking about it made her want to cry. Had he had an accident? She hated not having a phone!

Then Alice remembered the radio. She dashed to the kitchen and cranked it up. She listened for a half-hour, until the bad news started to repeat itself. Saint-Hyacinthe had no power. The airport and the train station were closed.

The bridges were closed.

Uncle Henri wasn't coming. *Couldn't* come.

Now Alice did cry. She crawled into bed, cuddled Juniper, and sobbed. Daddy thought she was at the farm. He probably wasn't going to come home. What was she going to do? Alice cried herself to sleep.

She woke up, disoriented, a few hours later. She was starting to lose track of time. For a girl whose whole life was ruled by the clock, it was almost scary not to know if it was six o'clock or eight o'clock or ten o'clock. Did it really matter?

It had been a good cry, a needful cry. Alice felt better with it out of her system. Now she was ready to take charge, keep fed, keep warm, look after the house. Dad hadn't noticed because he was used to working outside, but the house was really, really cold. He also hadn't noticed that she was wearing her winter jacket inside. How cold was it going to get? Alice got out of bed and went straight to the thermostat. Six degrees. The house had only lost two degrees during the day when the outside temperature had been around zero, but with night coming, how low would it go? Could the house hit three degrees? Next question – could she survive inside a refrigerator?

It was weird to think that the fridge and freezer were thawing out while she was freezing. That gave Alice an idea. She put on her boots and carefully made her way out to the backyard, holding on to the side of the house so she wouldn't slip. With a big kitchen spoon, she broke through the ice to the snow below and scooped it into a bowl. She broke off all the icicles she could reach and put them in the bowl too. Back inside she put the snow and ice into the freezer and the fridge. There. That should help hold the food a little longer.

Alice thought about her Dad sleeping in a tent and it gave her an idea. She went into the garage, dragging out the box of camping gear. She was a little surprised they still had it – she and Dad hadn't gone camping since Mom died. She pulled out the tent and all three sleeping bags. There was even a little battery-operated lantern in there. Alice took that too. Dragging all the gear into the living room, she set up her new base camp. Reckoning that her body heat would keep the inside of the tent warmer than the rest of the house, Alice wrestled with the springy tent poles. Finally, it was up, sitting right in the middle of the living room. She arranged the sleeping bags inside. She retrieved her book from her bedroom and put it next to the lantern. She made a cup of tea from the water in the thermos.

There, Alice thought. I'm tough. I'm a survivor.

DAY THREE
Wednesday, January 7, 1998

An Accident

ALICE WOKE WITH A START. EVERYTHING WAS silent now, but there'd been a noise. A really big noise. She sat up, only to bump her head against a soft web. She put her arms out. She was in some kind of a cocoon. It took her two full seconds to remember that she was sleeping in her tent in the living room. Two full seconds of panic. Alice took a deep breath. Storm. Ice. Cold. Tent.

Tree.

The noise had to have come from another tree falling down. It had made enough noise to wake her up, so it had to have fallen close by. Too close not to look, but Alice didn't want to leave the safety of her tent. Sighing, she crawled out anyway and made her way to the sliding doors in the dining room. There was just a hint of dawn on the horizon; it was probably about six in the morning. Alice peered into the back-yard. She'd known in her heart that it was their maple. It had split at the fork. The far half had crashed right through the Tickle Lady's roof.

Alice felt paralyzed. Was Mrs. Hartley dead? Their houses were mirror images of each other, which meant that the hole in the roof was right on top of the master bedroom on the second floor. If Mrs. Hartley had been asleep like a normal person would be at that hour, she was surely dead. Stabbed through the heart by a maple dagger.

Had any of the other neighbours heard the noise? Alice didn't see any flashlights or lanterns bobbing down the street to investigate. Maybe she should try to wake somebody up to go over and check. She put on more layers of warm clothing, then her boots. Carefully she made her way down the front steps and tried to wake the neighbour across the street.

"Mr. Carlisle, Mr. Carlisle!" she shouted. "Wake up!" Nothing happened. Alice tried the next house, and the next. It looked like all the other families had left, gone to stay with friends or relatives that had power, or at a hotel, like the Thibeau family. Which didn't help her one bit. She tried one more house, then gave up. Her shouting alone should have wak-ened the whole street by now, if there'd been anybody to hear. Alice cautiously walked back to stand in front of Mrs. Hartley's house. She had to go in.

The front door was locked, of course. So was the back door. The kitchen was on ground level. Alice shone her lantern in the window. What a mess! The tree had fallen through the bedroom on the top floor and crashed right down into the kitchen below. There were branches everywhere, along with great chunks of plaster from the ceiling, pieces of hardwood flooring that had fallen from the bedroom and bits of drywall from the damaged walls. Alice lifted the lantern higher. She thought she saw something.

It was Mrs. Hartley. She was lying on the floor amidst all the debris. And she wasn't dead. Her foot was twitching.

Alice was petrified. She needed help to break into the house and get Mrs. Hartley out, and she needed an ambulance to take her away, and she needed her dad — right now! But she wasn't going to get any of those things, not without a phone. She was on her own.

"Mrs. Hartley, I see you!" Alice yelled through the window. "I'm coming!"

But how?

Alice ran back to her house, taking care not to fall. Now would not be a good time to give herself a concussion. In the garage, she got an old car mat and Dad's axe; it was the heaviest thing she could find. She took them back to Mrs. Hartley's. Holding the axe like a baseball bat, Alice swung it towards the window. It hit the window, but didn't break it. How could that be? That kid had put a ball through the window from right across the street. Maybe the Tickle Lady had put in special reinforced bulletproof, axeproof windows after that. Yeah, right. The axe was just too heavy. Alice couldn't put enough oomph into the swing.

Returning the axe to the garage, Alice chose a hammer this time. At least she could really swing it. Back at the window, Alice closed her eyes tightly and swung with all her might. She felt the hammer go through the glass and was so surprised she nearly let go and let it fly right through the hole with all the broken pieces. The sound was just like that of the ice falling from the trees, only louder and sharper and a whole lot uglier. Alice could hardly believe she had broken a window on purpose.

The jagged hole wasn't big enough. Alice had to use the hammer to knock all the sharp bits away from the edges of the window before she had an opening big enough to crawl through. She laid the car mat over the edge, hoisted herself up and rolled into Mrs. Hartley's kitchen.

Alice rushed to Mrs. Hartley. "Are you all right?" she asked breathlessly.

After a brief silence, she heard a voice.

"What do you think, you fool girl? Do I look all right?"

Alice caught her breath. It really was the Tickle Lady and Alice was going to rescue her and then be tickled to death. The thought was so ridiculous that she started to laugh.

"You think this is funny?" demanded Mrs. Hartley in an outraged tone.

"No," replied Alice. "I was just so relieved you were alive. Nervous laughter, I guess."

"Hmmmph," snorted Mrs. Hartley. "Get me out of here."

Alice surveyed the mess. She'd have to be careful moving the old woman away from the branches. Every time Alice tried to move one out of the way, another shower of plaster came drifting down.

"Are you trying to totally destroy my house?"

"I think your house is already totally destroyed, Mrs. Hartley." Alice carefully extracted a few more branches, then gently dragged Mrs. Hartley away from the debris, helping her sit with her back against the dining room wall.

Alice took a look at the old woman. Her thin white hair, normally pinned into a bun at the nape of her neck, was hanging loose around her face and spattered with blood from a cut on her head. Her hair was really long, longer than Alice had imagined, but there was very little of it. Mrs. Hartley was practically bald. And skinny. She looks like a scrawny chicken, Alice thought unkindly. Good thing she's wearing so many layers, or else she'd be nothing but a bag of bones.

And of course, let's not forget those fingernails. Alice didn't want to look at them but curiosity won out. Ugh. There were even worse than the neighbourhood kids had described. Not so long as four inches, but thick and cracked and brownish. They didn't even look like nails. They reminded Alice of something else, but she couldn't quite remember what. Horns – cow horns – that's what! How could Mrs. Hartley let them get that way? It was disgusting. But then Alice noticed Mrs. Hartley's leg and her sympathy came back. The leg was badly cut and bleeding heavily.

"Go to the bathroom. There's a first aid kit in the bottom drawer," commanded Mrs. Hartley.

Alice brought the kit back to the dining room, and Mrs. Hartley talked her through the cleaning, disinfecting and bandaging of the cut. Alice tried her best to be gentle and Mrs. Hartley didn't complain once, but by the time she was finished the old lady was really pale. Alice was getting scared again.

"You have to take me to your house," said Mrs. Hartley. "The rain's pouring in. I'll freeze here."

Inwardly Alice groaned. Of course Mrs. Hartley was right, but she was the last person Alice would have chosen for company. And how to get her next door? Mrs. Hartley couldn't walk on that leg and Alice sure couldn't carry her, especially with all that ice. Alice thought for a moment, then said, "I'll be right back.

I've got an idea." After taking an afghan that had been on the living room sofa and wrapping it around Mrs. Hartley, Alice dashed back to her garage.

Alice rummaged through the old sports equipment until she found her old toboggan. She smiled as she remembered how much fun it had been sliding down the hill in the schoolyard. It would do just fine. Alice went outside to the backyard, dragging the toboggan. The fence was partially crushed by the maple. With a little help, Alice thought to herself as she pulled away a few more boards, I can make the opening big enough for the toboggan. Alice had to remove six more boards before she could be sure. Dad won't mind, she thought to herself. It's broken already.

Back at Mrs. Hartley's, Alice half-lifted, half-rolled the old lady onto the toboggan. "Hold on," she warned. Mrs. Hartley held tightly to the rope handles on each side. "I'll take you through the backyards; only one step out your back door and one step up mine. The toboggan can handle it if you hold on tight."

Alice took the lead rope and pulled, trying not to let the toboggan slide sideways as she negotiated her way around the branches and out the back door. The step was easy, but getting through the fence wasn't. Mrs. Hartley helped by holding on to what was left of the fence and pushing while Alice pulled. And together, they did it. Alice was astounded. Her idea had actually worked!

Alice settled Mrs. Hartley on her living room sofa and covered her with one of the sleeping bags.

"Finally," the old woman grumbled. "I'm half-frozen!"

Ungrateful bag of bones, thought Alice. *Maybe I should have left her there.* But good manners won out.

"Would you like a warm drink?" Alice asked. "I can make you one." Mrs. Hartley nodded imperiously, so Alice went outside to start up the barbecue. Dawn was over and the sun was up, making the ice sparkle. "Sure," Alice addressed the icicles all around her. "Go ahead and look pretty. We still hate you!"

Mrs. Hartley seemed grateful for the tea. She actually thanked Alice, wonder of wonders, and her whole body seemed to relax when she took the first sip. But by the time the cup was empty, Mrs. Hartley's hands were shaking. That didn't look good. Mrs. Hartley could barely put the cup and saucer down on the coffee table. Alice had to help her. Was that shock?

"Are you okay?" asked Alice, worried.

"Of course I am!" Mrs. Hartley tried to look fierce but couldn't pull it off, which made Alice worry even more.

"In case you haven't noticed, I'm old. I prefer not to have trees fall on me and be dragged around on a sled," Mrs. Hartley went on. "I'm tired. I'm going to sleep." With that, Mrs. Hartley lay down on the couch. Her whole body seemed to melt with fatigue and she fell asleep instantly. Alice wondered if that was a good idea, seeing as the old lady might be in shock and had also hit her head. Hadn't she heard you were supposed to keep people awake if they got a bonk on the head?

Alice didn't know much about first aid. She *did* know that she didn't want to wake Mrs. Hartley up again. She moved her tent close to the sofa then climbed back into it, leaving the flap open so she could keep an eye on Mrs. Hartley. She was exhausted. She had broken a window, performed a rescue and now she was babysitting the Tickle Lady. How weird was that?

DAY FOUR
Thursday, January 8, 1998

S OPHIE WOKE TO A QUIET, COLD HOUSE. THAT meant no generator running and no parents. It also meant she'd better get up and tend to the wood stove to make sure it didn't go out and then check Sébastien's schedule to find out when they were supposed to have power again. Life had all of a sudden become very complicated.

It had taken her, Sébastien and Maman four hours to get the milking done yesterday afternoon using the generator. When they had electricity, the job only took two. Their cows had to be milked twice a day, so that meant they needed the generator for eight hours a day. There were twenty-four hours in a day, so they could share with two other farms. Each farm got the generator for four hours then passed it to the next family.

But that wasn't the only scheduling problem. Since

the milk couldn't be kept cool unless the generator was working, milk trucks had to pick up the milk immediately after milking, or it would spoil. But in order to pump the milk from the coolers into the refrigerated milk trucks, you needed power. And once full, the milk trucks could only take their milk to refrigeration plants that also had power. Some of the processing plants had closed because they didn't have enough generator power to keep all the milk cool, so the trick was to find a processing plant still open so the milk truck could be sent to the right place. The whole process took a lot of coordination, making sure there was generator power available every step of the way.

Strangely, or maybe not so strangely, Sébastien had become an expert in organization. Even though he was just this weird little nine-year-old, he seemed to be able to figure out all the logistics of what equipment should be in what place and where it should go next. He had a list of farmers, a list of equipment, a time chart and even a map of the farms. Once he'd figured out what should go where, he called Papa on the cell phone and told him what to do. Papa took it from there. Maybe it was all those video games that had taught him how to strategize. Whatever it was, Sébastien seemed to have come a long way from worrying about a *loup-garou* attack. It cracked Sophie up when she thought of all the people who unknowingly were following the instructions of a nine-year-old in the middle of a crisis. And although she would never in a million years admit it, she was actually kind of proud of him.

Sophie got out of bed but didn't bother with her housecoat. She was already wearing three layers, and the kitchen would be warm. She made her way down to the kitchen, stoked the stove and put some water on to heat. She checked the clock on the wall – battery operated, thank goodness. They had never lived by the clock before, but they sure had to now. It was 7:00 a.m. She checked Sébastien's schedule. He had drawn a huge chart on the back of a big sheet of left-over Christmas paper. With different crayons he had coloured in the three farms, calling them Farm A, Farm B, and Farm C. He'd added the generator and the milk trucks. Sophie had added cooking, laundry, feeding the cows and cleaning the barn to the schedule. They had the generator from noon to four in the afternoon and from midnight to four in the morning. That meant she and Sébastien had to feed the cows and bring in more wood for the stove before then. When Papa and Maman came back with the generator, they had to be ready to go.

Sébastien came into the kitchen, dark hair sticking up all over his head. He immediately checked the time, then his schedule, just as Sophie had. Helping himself to a bowl of cold cereal, Sébastien planned out the day, making colour-coded adjustments here and there. Then he called Papa.

"*Allo, allo,*" he said. "Papa, are you on schedule?" Sébastien nodded while he listened, making a few notes on his chart. "*D'accord, c'est bien!*" Sophie rolled her eyes as he hung up the phone with a flourish.

"More," he demanded, holding his bowl out for a refill. "Little tyrant," responded his sister, as she filled the bowl.

Sébastien fixed his green eyes on her face. "You're nicer than you used to be," he said, narrowing his eyes. "Why?"

"Because you're smarter than you used to be," she shot back. "You haven't talked about a *loup-garou* since Monday."

"*Loup-garous* don't like the rain," replied Sébastien as he slopped orange juice over his cereal. Sophie groaned. So much for feeling proud of her weird little brother.

After breakfast they headed out to the main barn. Feeding all the cows was a big job. Each cow ate about twenty-five pounds of hay and twenty pounds of grain every day. They also drank eight gallons of water, but there was nothing Sophie and Sébastien could do about the water until the generator arrived to work the water pump. Luckily there was still a little left in the trough. The cows were milling about the free-stall barn where they were spending most of their time because of the awful weather. It made the barn pretty hot and stinky, and there was an awful lot of manure. The cow manure was usually removed by an alley scraper but the scraper, just like everything else, was run by electricity. Sébastien would have to shovel.

Sophie attached the hay trailer to the tractor. Then she loaded some bales of hay to feed the cows. It should have been silage, but silage was stored in the tall silos behind the barn and it took power to get it out. So hay was the only option. Sophie drove into the centre aisle of the free-stall barn. Using a pitchfork, she put a small pile of hay in front of each cow's stall. Immediately heads began to stick out through the metal rungs of the barriers as the cows reached for a mouthful.

When the cows in the main barn were content, Sébastien went back to the house to make adjustments to his schedule and Sophie went to visit Mélisande. Adalie mooed gently as soon as she saw Sophie. The calf came to nuzzle Sophie's hand, looking up at her with huge soft brown eyes.

"You are so beautiful!" crooned Sophie as she crouched down to rub Mélisande's velvety nose. "Has Adalie been giving you good feeds? Have you got lots of milk inside you?"

As if in answer, Mélisande moved away and began butting Adalie's udder. She found a teat and latched on. Little rivulets of thin, white milk began to drip from the edges of Mélisande's mouth as she sucked. Sophie smiled. "It looks like you're doing just fine."

Outside chores done, at least as many as could be done without power, Sophie went back into the house to wait. When the generator arrived, practically an army of people arrived with it. All of Saint-Hyacinthe was following the power.

Just a few minutes after noon a parade of vehicles began to snake down their lane. First was the tractor dragging the generator. Papa was driving. Behind him came Maman in the truck. The back of the truck was full of brown grocery bags. Behind her was the milk truck. And behind the milk truck came the neighbours in various pickups and four-wheel drives. The farm with the generator not only had power for their animals, but also had power for people. Lights went on, TVs and radios worked, furnaces kept houses warm, and water tanks, after a little catch-up time, gushed with hot water. In the middle of a blackout, everybody shared.

Sébastien ticked off the arrival of the generator and the milk truck. Mission accomplished for Farm A. Then he grabbed a clipboard, ready to sign people up for the shower schedule. Sophie made sure there was a stack of clean towels in the bathroom. The neighbours parked all higgledy-piggledy in the yard, leaving just enough room for the milk truck to escape once it finished pumping all their milk from the bulk tank into the refrigerated truck. Papa hooked the generator up to the pole and flicked the switch. Lights! Heat!

Action! The men headed for the barn. More hands made the milking and the watering and the cleaning go faster. The women headed for the house. They dutifully signed up on Sébastien's shower schedule, and then descended on the kitchen while the water reheated. Dough was kneaded, vegetables were chopped and casseroles prepared. Sébastien picked up his video camera and made himself annoying.

"This is Madame Boisvert making broccoli casserole. She always makes it for the church potlucks. Too bad it has to have broccoli. Madame Boisvert, is that absolutely necessary? Can you add more bacon, *s'il vous plâit,* to disguise the taste?" Madame Boisvert shook her wooden spoon at him good-naturedly.

"This is Madame de Bellefeuille making her world-famous *tourtière!*" Madame de Bellefeuille was okay with the filming, except she didn't want Sébastien to capture her secret ingredient and of course, that's exactly what he tried to do. It was pretty funny, and all the neighbours knew Sébastien, so there were no hard feelings. Sébastien was just being Sébastien.

Two of Sophie's friends came with their parents, who had come to help with the milking. The three of them retreated to her bedroom, at least until they smelled biscuits baking and hightailed it back to the kitchen. The smells were heavenly. When the steaming casseroles were pulled from the oven to cool, the women cycled through the shower, trying to leave at least enough hot water for the men to use to wash up before they ate. The men came to the kitchen in shifts, and then went straight back to the barns.

Four hours later, after the last group of men had washed and eaten, the women divvied up the bread and the casseroles for each family to take home. Papa unhooked the generator and gave the tractor keys to the neighbour who owned Farm B. The pickups and four-wheel drives filled up with people and snaked back down the lane. Some of them went back to their own homes to sleep and others went on to Farm B to help with the chores there. Maman cleaned the kitchen. Sébastien went back to his chart, studying the details of the next shift.

Sophie collected all the dirty towels to go into the washing machine at midnight when they next got the generator, and then slumped down on a kitchen chair with a tired smile. Really, the power outage was an awful lot of fun.

"Girl? Girl! Wake up!"

Alice rolled over in her sleeping bag. She was so warm. Except for her nose, which felt like a small icicle. She poked that icicle out of the tent.

"Yes, Mrs. Hartley?" she asked groggily. "Do you need something?"

Mrs. Hartley was sitting up on the sofa. She raised her eyebrows. "Girl, I need a lot of things, most of which I can't have. Right now, I need my medicine. It's in my backyard."

"Where?" asked Alice. She was hardly awake.

"My backyard. I never took you to be stupid, girl. Wake up!"

Alice crawled out of the tent. "Why is your medicine in your backyard? Where in your backyard?" Alice was trying, but this was a little weird.

"I'm diabetic," said Mrs. Hartley slowly, enunciating each word as if she was speaking to an idiot. "My insulin has to be kept cold. How cold is your fridge these days, girl?" demanded the old lady.

"Well, pretty cold," replied Alice tartly. She was awake now. "I filled it with ice and snow."

"Hmmm," said Mrs. Hartley. "Well, I said you weren't stupid. The insulin is right outside the back door, stuck in a snowbank. I need one vial marked "40" and one marked "50." And I need my diabetic kit. It's in the downstairs medicine cabinet. And if you don't want me passing out on you, you'd better get it NOW!"

Alice hurried. A passed-out Mrs. Hartley would not be a good thing to have in her living room. She shrugged into one of Dad's coats and went out the back door. The insulin was easy to find, the diabetic kit not so much. Boy, the old lady took an awful lot of medicine! Alice took a quick look...she had more pill containers than a pharmacy. There were a couple of medical kits; one had a bunch of needles in it, and another had a couple of little electronic dohickeys with a whole bunch of tiny white strips of plastic. Alice wasn't sure which kit Mrs. Hartley needed, although the needles seemed a pretty good bet. She grabbed both. Luckily Mrs. Hartley hadn't passed out by the time she got back.

Mrs. Hartley used one of the electronic dohickeys to prick her finger and squeezed a big drop of blood on one of the plastic strips. Alice was horrified and fascinated all at once. The old lady stuck the bloody plastic thing in the other machine and it started to beep. When it finished beeping, Mrs. Hartley checked the readout on the machine. "Not good," she murmured to herself. She looked at the "40" vial. The liquid inside was too cold, nearly frozen. She couldn't draw it out of the vial. Mrs. Hartley gave the vial to Alice.

"Warm it up; roll it between your hands. You'll have more body heat than me."

Alice did what she was told, and then handed the vial back. Mrs. Hartley took one of the needles and inserted it into the vial. It was just like in the movies, when the bad guy fills a needle with poison to kill somebody. Alice watched with wide eyes as Mrs. Hartley lifted up her nightgown and stuck the needle right into her side. Gross, gross, and super gross!

"Is that what all diabetics have to do?" asked Alice when she had recovered from the sight of Mrs. Hartley's wrinkled stomach.

Mrs. Hartley fixed a look on Alice. Then she sighed. "If they're insulin dependent. Some people can just take pills, but not me."

"What will happen if you don't take the insulin?"

"I'll die," said Mrs. Hartley simply.

It was Alice's turn to stare at Mrs. Hartley. Wow. Then she had a horrible thought. "How much insulin is in your snowbank?"

Mrs. Hartley leaned back against the sofa and closed her eyes. "Two more days worth." Alice spent a minute taking in that little piece of information. Babysitting Mrs. Hartley was not going to be easy.

Alice escaped to the kitchen, promising to make some hot tea. She needed to think. All of a sudden, her plans for dealing with the cold and the dark and the loneliness had changed. Now she had Mrs. Hartley, who couldn't walk and was going to die in two days if Alice couldn't get her more medicine. Unbelievable. Were pharmacies even open? Could she get to one if they were? And didn't diabetics need special food? It wasn't like her kitchen was offering a lot of choice.

While Mrs. Hartley drank the tea, Alice asked her about the food thing. It wasn't so bad after all; Mrs. Hartley could eat tinned spaghetti and baked beans and they had lots of that kind of stuff. Mrs. Hartley gave her a list of the other drugs she needed from her house and Alice collected them all up in a plastic bag. She also brought over some of the non-perishable food from Mrs. Hartley's kitchen. So far, so good. They had a pretty good larder and Alice's barbecuing skills were improving. After a couple more hot drinks, Alice was pretty sure she could move on from boiling water and actually cook something.

They both napped after lunch. Alice left the tent flap open again. It seemed rude to zip the door shut with somebody else in the room. She woke to find Mrs. Hartley staring into the tent right at her. She could be really creepy sometimes. Alice glanced down at the nails. They were safely in Mrs. Hartley's lap. Unfortunately, the old lady noticed the glance.

"Worried I'm going to tickle you to death?" she said ominously.

Alice's jaw dropped. "You know that's what the kids say about you?"

"I'm not blind or deaf, girl. Course I know. Kept all of you off my property, didn't it?"

Alice didn't know how to respond. "So you don't like kids?"

Mrs. Hartley didn't answer. There was an uncomfortable silence. Alice decided to crank up the radio.

Montréal is a photographer's dream — the icy vistas are intensely beautiful. It is also being called a war zone. Today, thousands more head for shelters in Ontario and Québec after more freezing rain delays repair work and Hydro-Québec admits there can be no quick fix. Even Rideau Hall, the Governor-General's home in Ottawa, has no power.

Alice sighed and turned the radio off. Mrs. Hartley shot a look Alice's way.

"Does your Dad drink?"

"What?!" Alice was shocked. "He doesn't, but that's none of your business!"

"Don't get your knickers in a knot. I want to know if you have any alcohol in the house."

"So you drink?" asked Alice belligerently.

"Oh, for heaven's sake," exploded Mrs. Hartley. "Stop being so prickly, girl! Just because you think I'm a monster doesn't actually make me one! I'm worried about the toilets."

Alice just stared. This conversation was making no sense at all. Toilets? To her surprise, Mrs. Hartley's lips began to quiver. In another moment she was smiling and after that came a great big belly laugh. Alice shifted from wondering about toilets to wondering how such a scrawny body could make so much noise. Maybe Mrs. Hartley was a full-on lunatic.

"I got up to go to the bathroom while you were sleeping, girl," said Mrs. Hartley between chuckles. "Lucky it wasn't far away, because old ladies like me, well, we gotta go when we gotta go. I noticed your taps dripping. That's smart."

Alice, still bewildered, said, "My Uncle Henri told

me to do that."

"Whatever," said Mrs. Hartley. "Toilets have to be protected from freezing too. You need to pour in some anti-freeze, if you've got it. If not, liquor will work as long as it has a high alcohol content."

"How does that stop them from freezing?" asked Alice. Her head was still spinning but she was curious.

"Alcohol lowers the freezing point of water. It'll have to get a lot colder before the water freezes, which hopefully means your toilets won't crack."

"But how will we use the toilets? Won't we flush it all away?" asked Alice.

"I meant," Mrs. Hartley said in a long-suffering voice, "MY toilet. I won't be needing it for the foreseeable future."

"Oh," said Alice. "So, just so I have this straight, you want me to find my dad's alcohol and pour it down your toilet?"

Mrs. Hartley nodded. "You got it, girl."

Shaking her head, Alice went to the cupboard where her dad kept the alcohol. He didn't drink strong liquor, so all he had was a bunch of unopened gift bottles his workers had given him for Christmas. She called out the names to Mrs. Hartley, who told her which ones had the highest alcohol content, and then trudged them over to Mrs. Hartley's house. This babysitting job was beginning to feel like slave labour.

Once back at home, Alice couldn't help herself.

"How did you know about the alcohol thing?" she asked.

Mrs. Hartley hesitated for a moment, as if she didn't want to admit the truth. Then she looked Alice straight in the eye. "I know a lot of things," she said. "I used to be a schoolteacher."

"But that's impossible," cried Alice. "You hate kids!"

"Did I say that?"

Alice didn't answer.

"You know nothing about me," said Mrs. Hartley quietly. "Even though I've been your next-door neighbour since you were born."

Well, that's not all my fault, Alice thought. *It wasn't like you were very friendly.*

"I knew your mother, though," Mrs. Hartley continued. "You're not much like her."

Alice bristled. "I am so," she said angrily. "Everyone says so!"

"Oh, you look like her, all right. But your mother had a mind of her own. She and I had some good talks. I was really sorry when she got sick." Mrs. Hartley sounded wistful.

The Tickle Lady and her mom had been friends? This day was getting weirder and weirder.

"How's the skating going?"

Alice tensed. "Fine."

"And you like it?"

"Of course I do."

"I see you on TV sometimes," said Mrs. Hartley. "You're sure you like it?"

"Of course I like skating! I love skating!" Mrs. Hartley was making Alice mad. "Why else would I spend my whole life doing it? What – you think I skate because I *don't* like it?"

Mrs. Hartley was quiet for a minute. "I just can't tell," she finally replied. "Is it what you want to do, or what you think others want you to do?"

That made Alice really angry. "I want it!" she exploded.

"What do you want?"

"I want to be a star! I've worked hard. I'm the best; I deserve it!"

"You might be the best skater, girl. But you're not the best competitor. You fall all over the place, for heaven's sake," Mrs. Hartley said bluntly. "Maybe you should wait until you're older to enter competitions."

Alice was so furious she thought she might scream. How dare this old woman say that to her? "You think it's easy, having everybody watching you? You try it sometime! So, you think I should just wait around, let everybody else get ahead, and then come back and win? That shows you know nothing about it! My career will be ruined if I wait. You only get one chance!"

"Don't be ridiculous!" Mrs. Hartley shot back. "You're only twelve years old. You don't have a 'career,' and not a single decision you make today will ruin

your life. It'll only teach you how to make better decisions later. It's the decisions that you don't make that
will come back to haunt you." Mrs. Hartley and Alice
locked eyes, Alice's leaking the furious tears she
couldn't hold back.

A LOUD POUNDING ON THE DOOR shattered the
moment. "Anybody in there? Anybody home?"

Alice got up slowly to go to the door, still shaking
a little from the strong words lying uneasily in the
room. She peered through the peephole and reeled
back in shock when she saw two huge soldiers. She
opened the door a crack.

"Are you here alone? Is anybody with you?" the
bigger one demanded.

"Mrs. Hartley. Mrs. Hartley is here too," Alice
stammered.

"Can we come in?"

Alice led them to the living room. The soldiers
asked a lot of questions about how warm they were
keeping, if they had any food, how they were cooking
it and stuff. They checked the thermostat, which was
down to four degrees. They asked what had happened
to Mrs. Hartley's house, as if that wasn't fairly obvious.
They asked about Alice's dad. Mrs. Hartley told them
about her medicine. They asked her if she had family
who could take her in.

"I have a daughter outside of Montréal. I called

her Monday before the phones stopped working. She has friends staying with her. She said she didn't have room for me," Mrs. Hartley said quietly. Alice bit her lip. How awful. Mrs. Hartley was creepy and mean and really didn't know what she was talking about when it came to Alice's life, but surely she wasn't that bad.

The soldiers said they should both be evacuated to a shelter, Mrs. Hartley because she was sick and Alice because she was too young to be on her own and her house was too cold.

Alice turned wide eyes to Mrs. Hartley. "No, we have to stay here! My dad won't know where to find me!"

The shorter soldier touched Alice gently on the shoulder. "You can leave your dad a note. Tell him we're taking you to the Eaton Centre on St. Catherine Street. They've set up a shelter there. There's heat, food, cots and a pharmacy in the mall for medicine. I'll even put my name on the note so your dad knows who to contact if he can't find you."

Alice was unconvinced, but Mrs. Hartley seemed excited by the idea. "Will there be other people there?" she asked.

The big soldier smiled as if at a secret joke. "Oh yes, *Madame,* there will be other people."

The big one went to Mrs. Hartley's house to pack her a few things for the shelter. Mrs. Hartley acted like she was going on a holiday or something, telling him to find her best blouse, the one wrapped in tissue in the top drawer. The short soldier went through the house with Alice, preparing it to be alone. He laughed when she poured alcohol down the toilet, but agreed it was a smart thing to do. He pushed the barbecue into the garage for safekeeping and helped her check all the doors and windows. Alice wrote a note to her dad and put it on the kitchen table, anchored by the sugar bowl. The soldier suggested they empty the fridge and freezer and put all the contents outside in a green garbage bag.

"The food will all be spoiled by the time you get home and your fridge will need a big cleanup," the soldier said. "Might as well keep the mess outside." Then he said quietly, "You were very brave to help your friend as you did."

"She's not my friend," said Alice unkindly. "Just a neighbour. A tree fell on her — nobody would just leave her there!"

"You'd be surprised," said the soldier grimly.

In a half-hour, they were ready to go. Alice shouldered the backpack she had filled with overnight stuff, including Juniper and her cell phone, and took a last look at the living room. She hoped her dad wouldn't be mad. But she could hardly say no to a soldier, right? As the big one carried Mrs. Hartley out to the army truck, the other one taped a big "X" across the front door.

"What are you doing?" she asked him curiously.

"This tells the other soldiers that your house has

been abandoned and there are no dead bodies inside," he replied.

"Have people died in their houses?" asked Alice in horror.

"Oh yes," said the soldier matter-of-factly. "Some elderly people have frozen to death. Some houses have burnt down because people didn't mind their candles. Some died from carbon monoxide poisoning when they tried to cook on their camp stoves inside the house." Alice grimaced. That explained why Dad had been so fierce about the camp stove.

As they drove slowly down her street, driving up on the Thibeau's lawn to avoid the fallen maple, Alice saw a big "X" on every one of her neighbours' homes. Abandoned. What a lonely word.

Alice usually took the *Métro* when she went to the mall. It was nothing like the trip she was taking now. She and Mrs. Hartley stared out their windows. That radio announcer hadn't been kidding when he called Montréal a war zone. The army was everywhere and some of the soldiers were carrying guns. They were going house to house, pounding on doors. Big convoys of army trucks drove past, carrying more soldiers. It was eerily quiet. There should have been traffic and car horns and music. But the intermittent pounding and shouting were the only sounds, and the thick blanket of ice and snow muffled them. Every so often the sky lit up with a flash of blue. Alice jumped the first time.

"Another transformer blowing," explained the big soldier. "The power grid is breaking faster than they can fix it."

Tears filled Alice's eyes. Was Dad okay? When would she see him again? All along the road the utility poles had snapped. It looked like a giant had walked down the street and stomped on every single one. The ground looked like a snakepit, with thick black high-voltage wire lying coiled everywhere. But worst of all were the people. The few that were out looked like clowns. They were fat with layers of warm clothes and most sported hockey or bicycle helmets on top of their toques to protect themselves from falling ice. There was nothing amused in their expressions. Some looked frightened, others looked angry. All were bewildered. Their faces said, "How could this happen to *us?*"

It took a long time to get to St. Catherine Street. Two big rooms in the Eaton Centre Mall were full of army cots. The room they were taken to was right next to the movie theatre. Alice guessed the concrete rooms were normally used for storage, because the rest of the Eaton Centre Mall was full of stores and had a glass roof. There were *lots* of people. Mrs. Hartley smiled in anticipation.

Alice sucked in her breath. She couldn't stay there, she couldn't. She had to go home.

DAY FIVE
Friday, January 9, 1998

IT WAS STILL RAINING. SOPHIE TRIED TO PROTECT HER face from the stinging pellets of freezing rain as she slipped and slid from the house to the barn. Her flashlight batteries were wearing out and it was hard to see her way. As she grabbed the heavy metal door and heaved it sideways, Sophie switched off her flashlight for a moment and looked behind her. She had never experienced such complete darkness. There was not a glimmer of light, not a promise of light anywhere. She tried to think of all the words Alice would use to describe it. Alice was the one who liked words. Thick, inky, velvety, deep, palpable.

Sophie gave herself extra points for that last one. It was a good word, because the dark wasn't actually something you saw, it was something you felt. She shivered. Thinking about the dark like that freaked her out. She turned the flashlight back on.

The cows were restless. Steam was building up in the barn, making it uncomfortable for them to breathe. Should she lower the curtains to give them some ventilation? Or would they freeze? They were hungry and thirsty too, but she didn't want to feed them until she was sure she could water them, and she wasn't sure when she could do that. The generator was late.

Sophie had sent Sébastien to bed around one in the morning. He had been nearly frantic trying to call all the farms and rearrange the schedule. Sophie had tried to assure him that it wasn't his fault. The chores were just taking longer. All the farmers were getting tired and it was hard to work through the night. The whole process had slowed down, which meant the cows had to wait, like it or not. That put the cows off schedule too, and they didn't milk well. Sébastien needed to sleep. They all did.

Sophie wished Alice was here. It was weird, not being able to phone or email. What was she doing? Uncle Pete wasn't going to be able to work as many hours if he had to keep going home to check on Alice, make her supper and stuff. And Alice could be another pair of hands. She was actually good at milking cows now, although her first time had been sort of rocky. The memory made Sophie smile.

She'd wanted to teach Alice how to milk a cow the old-fashioned way. It just seemed like something everybody ought to know how to do. When Alice sat on the little stool, she was terrified that the huge cow would sit on her and crush her. Sophie knew it wouldn't. But when Alice tried to make the teats squirt out milk, the cow flicked its tail around and caught her right across the face. Not only that, it whipped her pearl earring right out of her ear. Alice was determined to get the earring back. But to do that she had to catch the tail and find the earring clinging to it. That tail – Sophie had to laugh when she thought of it. Cow's tails don't get shampooed on a regular basis. They can be kind of mucky. Alice had been horrified. But she got her earring back. Sophie had been proud of her.

She frowned. Those stupid bridges.

Sophie decided to lower the barn curtains a little, to balance ventilation with the cold. Good thing they had a hand-winch for that. Just about everything else on the farm needed electricity. Then she left, because her presence was raising the cows' expectations of being fed and she needed to know about the generator before she could start. She patted the cordless phone in her pocket, in case Maman called to say she was on her way home. Sophie decided to see if Mélisande was awake while she waited.

Mélisande was sleeping. She looked so peaceful. Sophie curled up on the hay beside her to share her warmth. There was nothing like a cow to keep you warm on a cold night. The sweet smell of hay, the tang of sour milk, the acrid undertone of urine – all were beautiful smells to Sophie. As she drifted off to sleep, she thought how strange it was that darkness had a feeling and warmth had a smell.

When the phone rang, Sophie jumped. It took her a moment to remember where she was. "Maman?" asked Sophie.

"*Oui, ma petite.* You were awake?"

"*Oui,* I'm with Mélisande. Are you on the way? The barn is steamy and the cows are restless," said Sophie urgently.

"*Je sais,*" replied Maman in a tired voice. "*Je sais.* We should be there in forty-five minutes, so you can start the hay. Is Sébastien asleep?"

"I put him to bed a couple of hours ago," answered Sophie. "He was upset about the schedule." Sophie could just imagine Maman shaking her head on the other end of the line.

"*Pauvre petit,*" she sighed. "His mind is so busy. He just can't let things go. Thank you for putting him to bed. As soon as we get home and get the milking started, you can go to bed too." Then she added, "*Merci,* Sophie. You are doing a wonderful job." Then she was gone.

Sophie smiled. Why wouldn't she do a good job? The cows were her family too. Grateful to be able to actually do something at long last, Sophie flicked on her flashlight and once again did battle with the storm. As she manoeuvred the tractor towards the feed, she was sure she felt the wind picking up. The howling was more deep-seated and seemed to whip the pellets of ice with greater viciousness into her face. She hoped she was wrong. Wind would tear more wires out of the sky. It was the last thing they needed.

ALICE SAT ON THE FOAMIE SHE HAD BEEN assigned, her knees to her chest, her arms squeezing them as close to her body as they could go. She hated this place. Each foamie was placed just two feet away from some stranger. Her neighbour on one side was a snotty-nosed kid who never stopped crying. On the other side was a burly man who not only snored but had unbelievably bad body odour. Their whole corner stank of sweat and farts and dirty diapers. Mrs. Hartley had done much better. Because she was old and sick, she got one of the Red Cross cots in a special section for old people.

It wasn't just the noise and the smell that was keeping Alice awake. She was afraid. The sleeping rooms had concrete ceilings but the rest of the Eaton Centre had a glass roof. Right next to the centre was a tall office tower and huge chunks of ice were falling off the tower, right onto the glass roof. What if the ice broke the roof, and it shattered on top of them?

Alice wasn't the only one who was worried. The

shelter staff didn't want to move all the people, but
when ice actually broke through the roof, sending
glass down onto the escalators, they made an
announcement. Everybody had to go to a different
shelter. Alice couldn't believe it. How would her dad
ever find her?

As shelter volunteers moved through the rows,
telling people to pack their stuff, Alice jumped up and
grabbed one of them by the arm.

"Please, if we have to move anyway, can I go
home? I could take a taxi. I do it all the time. I even
know what driver to call. Guillaume knows me, and
he knows where I live. My dad won't be able to find
me if I go to a different shelter!"

"No," said the volunteer wearily. "You're registered
with us. We can't let you go without an adult signing
for you. Don't worry, your dad will find out what's
happened. Why isn't he with you, anyway?"

"He works for Hydro," replied Alice.

"Ah," said the volunteer. "That explains it. I wish
him luck with this mess. In the meantime, go get
your stuff."

Alice decided to move with Mrs. Hartley. She
didn't know anybody else, and anyway, the old lady
seemed way less grumpy than she had been. She actually seemed to enjoy the people in the shelter,
although Alice couldn't believe how. Going to the old
people's section, she helped Mrs. Hartley pack up her

things and stayed with her as they waited to be transported to Place Ville-Marie, just down the road. While they waited, a man from the St-Viateur Bagel Shop came in with a huge box that smelled delicious. Alice jumped up to say hello.

"Maurice! *Comment ça va?*"

Maurice smiled at Alice. "Good – we've got a generator! Are you keeping warm? Where's your dad?" Alice chatted with Maurice as she helped him hand out hot bagels to the people at the shelter. The heavenly smell had drawn a crowd, but Alice made sure she saved one for Mrs. Hartley.

After a bagel and the short ride in an army truck to Place Ville-Marie, Alice felt better. Place Ville-Marie was a nicer shelter as far as she was concerned, because it was an office building and there weren't so many people in each room. The building was forty-seven stories tall, so nothing was likely to fall on its roof. She'd never been in any of the offices in the tower before, but she'd been shopping at some of the cool stores in the underground *Galerie* before. After she was settled in an office on the thirty-eighth floor with just thirteen people, Alice went to find Mrs. Hartley again. A nurse was with her, helping her use the little machine to check her blood sugar. The nurse checked the readout and measured out a shot of insulin. Then she checked Mrs. Hartley's leg.

"You'll have to be really careful of this, *Madame.*

You know that diabetics have a hard time healing wounds in their lower extremities and the cut could get infected. Let the volunteers know if you see any redness or puffiness."

Mrs. Hartley said she would. Then the nurse looked at Mrs. Hartley's hands. "I can help you with those nails," she said. "I have my special clippers."

"Would you?" asked Mrs. Hartley. "They are too thick for me to cut and sometimes it's hard for me to get out to have them clipped."

So Mrs. Hartley couldn't help that her nails were long. Alice blushed. She should have known, if she'd thought about it. Who would want to go around looking like that and having people make fun of you? Alice felt a little ashamed. Not that she'd actually ever made fun of Mrs. Hartley to her face, but she'd done it in her head. Alice supposed it wasn't really much different.

Mrs. Hartley didn't say a word about it to Alice. After the nurse left, they turned on the television. Lots of the offices had television sets. Alice had almost forgotten what it was like to watch TV, even though it had only been five days. She plopped down on the end of Mrs. Hartley's cot to watch the news. The headlines were awful.

Montréal is paralyzed! Soldiers have been called in to help the millions of people hit by the worst ice storm in living memory. The outlook looks grim after four days and seven deaths. With eastern Ontario and Québec already in chaos, the Atlantic provinces are now bracing for the storm.

Six hundred soldiers were sent to the disaster zone today and 3,500 more are on their way as 3.5 million people try to survive without power. A state of emergency has been declared in Montréal, Kingston, Brockville, Cornwall and many other municipalities. One hundred thousand people have taken refuge in shelters. Even Ottawa, the nation's capital, has declared a state of emergency, the first in its history.

The disaster was made worse this morning when five hundred hydro towers in Vankleek Hill were flattened by ice, shutting down Montréal's subway lines for the first time ever and destroying two of the five power lines that feed the city. The stability of the power grid hangs by a thread. An exhausted power worker spoke to our correspondent earlier.

"We fix one block, move to another and the one we just left loses power again because more branches fall on the line."

Three thousand Hydro-Québec employees are working sixteen-hour shifts to try to fix the power grid. Soon they will be joined by a thousand linemen from the United States who are already on their way to volunteer assistance to Canadians.

Alice grinned at Mrs. Hartley, who grinned right back, false teeth and all. "They're coming to help Dad!" Alice cried.

Here is the situation as it stands now. Virtually all schools in eastern Ontario and western Québec are closed. Highway 417 is closed. Train service has been cancelled from Toronto to points east. Most flights are cancelled. Schools, colleges and universities are closed, as are banks, government offices and hundreds of stores, restaurants and offices. Emergency wards are overflowing with more than one hundred cases of carbon monoxide poisoning as people try to heat their homes with camp stoves and other devices. All elective surgery has been cancelled. Another 1,000 shelters have opened in Montréal. Police are requesting everyone to stay off the roads, which are "nothing more than skating rinks or obstacle courses."

Rural areas have been especially hard hit. The Premier of Ontario has issued a cross-Canada appeal for generators, desperately needed by dairy farmers to power their livestock feeding and milking equipment.

Alice caught her breath. "Mrs. Hartley, I didn't think about that! About the cows, I mean. Yesterday my radio said that Saint-Hyacinthe was completely without power, and that's where my cousin lives.

They've got fifty cows! What are they going to do?"

"Do they have a generator?" asked Mrs. Hartley. "Some farmers do."

Alice let out a big breath. "Of course, they do. I forgot. That's what Uncle Henri told me when he called the other day. He said he was coming to get me because even if their power went out they'd be okay because they had a generator. But then the bridges closed, so – here I am."

"Lucky for me," said Mrs. Hartley gruffly.

"I guess," Alice smiled. Then she took the smile back. She was still sore about what the old woman had said back at the house. But not as sore as she thought she would feel. Why was it okay to be with Mrs. Hartley after their argument? Usually, Alice avoided people who made her feel bad. But with Mrs. Hartley, it was different. Alice shrugged her shoulders. The ice storm was making everything feel weird.

"I should try calling Sophie to tell her where I am," she told Mrs. Hartley. "Dad's cell is dead, but my aunt and uncle might still have a phone."

Alice went to her cot and got her backpack. Pulling out her cell phone, she dug deep in the bag to get the charger. She couldn't find it. She dumped everything out of the backpack. Alice couldn't believe it. She'd remembered the phone but not the charger. How could she be so dense?

At lunchtime, Alice helped hand out sandwiches

and juice boxes. "Where did these come from?" she asked a volunteer named Jean-Michel.

"Different places," he replied. "For the past couple of days we've been getting pretty great food from supermarkets and restaurants because it made more sense to give it away than let it spoil on the shelves. You know, there was this one guy who walked up to a policeman and handed the cop the keys to his grocery store. 'I'm taking my family out of the city,' he said. 'Take whatever you need.' Isn't that cool?"

That was really cool. "I heard that some people are stealing generators," she said.

"Oh yeah, lots of people are doing that. And there's been looting at stores and break-and-enters at abandoned houses. A whole lot of people are going to get a surprise when they get home!"

Alice frowned. Well, nothing she could do about her abandoned house. "Why?" she asked. "I mean, it's pretty obvious that we've got a big problem here – why make it worse?"

"That's easy," replied Jean-Michel. "People are selfish. They look at a problem and ask 'What's in it for me?' They don't ask, 'How can I help?' There will always be scumbags, kid. Get used to it."

Alice didn't think she wanted to get used to it.

"How can I help?" she asked him.

He laughed. "So, you don't want to be a scumbag, eh?" Alice laughed too. Jean-Michel looked her up and down. "You're sure I can trust you?" he asked more seriously. Alice nodded.

"The worst thing right now is boredom," he said. "Parents are worried and upset. They're not paying attention to their kids. The kids aren't used to all this free time and they don't know what to do. Do you think you could read to them for a while?"

"Sure," said Alice, "but I don't have any books with me." Thinking of Guillaume, she added, "I know a few stories that I can tell without books, but not many."

"Not a problem," replied Jean-Michel with a grin. He reached into his pocket and pulled out a set of keys that he dangled enticingly in front of Alice's eyes. "The keys to the kingdom!"

"What are you talking about?"

"You know the bookstore that's down in the *Galerie,* the underground mall beneath this building? Well, I work there. That's why I'm here. When the weather got bad I decided to stay here instead of go home. But there's no point in opening up the store. There are no customers and we shouldn't waste the power right now anyway." Jean-Michel handed her the keys. "Go downstairs and pick out some books the kids would like."

"You're kidding, right?" asked Alice, aghast. "I can really just go and unlock the bookstore and take some books?"

"Not take – borrow for a good cause. Just make

sure you keep them in mint condition so my boss doesn't find out!"

Alice grabbed the keys and ran before Jean-Michel could change his mind. She couldn't believe her luck. The underground mall was lit, but only dimly because the stores were closed. It was a little freaky to be there all alone. The only sounds Alice could hear were her footsteps: no music, no cell phones, no people talking. An image of Sébastien's *loup-garou* flashed into her head before she could stop it. The sound of its claws clicked ominously on the shiny linoleum behind her... Alice whirled around, then rolled her eyes. Ridiculous. There was no monster. Except maybe for the storm, and it wasn't inside the *Galerie*.

Shaking her head, she unlocked the door to the bookstore. Keys to the kingdom! Alone in a bookstore – it was like a dream come true! Alice went right to the kids' section. She'd start with Robert Munsch. *Mortimer* was her favourite, but maybe *50 Below Zero* was more appropriate for an ice storm? And how about *Magie d'un jour de pluie* – some rainy day magic would be just the ticket. They were all fun to read out loud, although the French kids would probably laugh at her atrocious accent. Sophie always did. And *Miss Rumphius;* she loved that book. *Zoom at Sea* and *Boy Soup* and *Pas de taches pour une girafe* would make everybody laugh. She loved *The Dragon's Pearl,* and...Alice grabbed at the book: *Mrs. Piggle Wiggle!*

Her own copy was long gone. *Jacob Two-Two and the Hooded Fang* and *The Nose from Jupiter* would be good if she got some older kids. She didn't want to stop, but her arms filled eventually.

Carefully Alice locked up the store and rattled the door to double-check. Carrying her treasures to the elevator, she had a little bounce in her step. Five days ago all she could think about was the skating competition, but that worry seemed very small now in comparison with everything else that was happening. Who would have thought on Monday that she'd be spending her Friday night not practicing at the arena but raiding an underground bookstore and playing librarian to a bunch of kids she didn't even know?

SOPHIE AND SÉBASTIEN STOOD SIDE BY SIDE at the window, looking anxiously down the lane. Where were Maman and Papa? Sébastien's schedule was completely falling apart. Sophie was having a hard time convincing him that it wasn't his fault.

"I'd better go check the cows again," said Sophie worriedly. She pulled on her outdoor clothes for about the millionth time. She'd put her mitts and boot liners by the wood stove but they still weren't dry. There was nothing worse than wet boots. Sighing, she put them on anyway. Outside, the weather was even worse, if that was possible. The wind was whipping around the corner of the barn, catching her full in the face and flinging icy rain into her eyes. Would it ever stop?

The cows were starting to bawl. The barn was stuffy, their udders were full and they were thirsty. The floor was covered with manure. Sophie carefully operated the hand-winch to lower the wall curtains for more ventilation, then grabbed a shovel and a wheelbarrow. Slowly she worked her way down the barn, shovelling manure into the wheelbarrow, cleaning up as best she could.

Just then she heard the telltale clatter of the tractor. They were home! Sophie raced back to the main barn to get the first ten cows in place to start milking. Maman climbed out of the truck to help. In minutes, Sébastien joined them. They all three worked feverishly and the first lot were cleaned and ready by the time Papa had the generator hooked up and flicked the switch. Power surged through the barn. The ventilation fans began to turn. Sébastien manned the water pump. Maman and Sophie moved up and down, speaking quietly to the cows, calming them. Everybody had a job, but poor Papa looked like he was ready to fall over. He had dark circles under his eyes and he hadn't shaved, so he was all bristly. Maman sent him to bed and he was so tired he didn't even argue.

"Papa is exhausted. All the farmers are trying to do the work of ten men and they can't keep it up," explained Maman. "Your help means a lot to him. When we drove in, he noticed that you had protected the woodpile and he was really pleased."

"Protected?" Sophie exchanged a glance with Sébastien. "We just brought it closer to the house so the wood would be easier to get. Why do we have to protect it?"

A black look passed over Maman's face. "Because people are stealing wood, that's why. Do you know that there are volunteers outside the *Triangle Noir,* the Triangle of Darkness they are calling us now, who are working for hours out in the freezing cold, cutting their own wood and bringing it to us to help us stay warm, and that lazy good-for-nothings are stealing that wood? People who have power but can't be bothered getting their own wood? People who are reselling the wood at high prices? *C'est terrible!* It makes me sick!"

They were shocked. But it was clear from the look on Maman's face that she wasn't making it up. "Why were you so late?" asked Sébastien. "We were so worried."

"I'm sorry, *mon petit,*" said Maman. "We took the generator for a detour to the Champlain farm."

"Why?" asked Sophie curiously. "They don't have cows, they have pigs. Pigs don't have to be milked." Sébastien giggled. Milk a pig?!

"It is worse for the pig farmers, Sophie," explained Maman wearily. "They need more ventilation in their barns than we do. If they don't have ventilation, even for an hour, the pigs start to die. Monsieur Champlain called us when his generator broke down. We finished at Farm C as fast as we could and took the generator over, but he'd already lost a good number of animals."

This was even more shocking than the wood story. Geneviève Champlain was in Sophie's class at school. She was going to be devastated.

"We cleared his barns as best we could, but I couldn't leave the generator, not with our cows waiting. He called the army. They're going to try to get him help. But he's not the only one in trouble." Maman sighed wearily.

Sophie looked closely at Maman. She looked nearly as tired as Papa. "Why don't you go to bed too, Maman?" said Sophie. "Everything's running. Sébastien and I can look after things for a bit."

"Mais non!" cried Maman. "There are too many cows to be milked. It will take all three of us."

"We can do it, Maman," said Sophie earnestly. She looked at Sébastien, who nodded vigorously. "Really we can."

"C'est sûr?" asked Maman. She sighed. *"Merci, mes enfants. Je suis très fatiguée."* Maman stumbled off after Papa. Sophie looked at Sébastien.

"I'm worried," she said. "They're too tired to work. They might have an accident with the machinery or something. We've got to let them sleep as long as they can. Can you arrange for the milk truck?"

"Mais oui," agreed Sébastien. "I'll make my voice deep, so they think it's Papa calling!"

Sophie looked around the milking parlour.

Everything was running smoothly. The cows were content. She wandered up and down the rows, speaking softly to the animals. What would she do if she lost them? She couldn't imagine having a disaster like the Champlains. She would just want to die.

Sébastien came tearing into the barn, hatless and coatless.

"The phones, the phones," he panted. "They're not working! And the cell is dead. I plugged it into the charger but it still won't work. I can't get through to the milk truck!"

"Slow down, Sébastien, breathe, for heaven's sake," said Sophie, but her mind was racing. No milk truck meant no pickup meant spoiled milk. Not a disaster. Not worth waking her parents because there was nothing they could do. The truck would come or it wouldn't. If the milk spoiled, so be it. *Don't cry over spilt milk,* Sophie told herself. The important thing was keeping the cows healthy.

Sophie went back to murmuring to the cows and her soft voice served to soothe Sébastien as well. When the first ten cows were done, the two of them put their milking gloves on to give the teats their final clean. Sophie pushed the button to release the finished cows. Sébastien was already herding the next ten into the milking parlour. As the cows took their places, Sophie and Sébastien worked as hard as they could to clean all the teats and hook up the cows by themselves. When the milk started flowing, Sébastien gave Sophie a high-five.

They'd done it – no parents required! Sophie had to smile at his enthusiasm. He wasn't such a bad little kid, not really.

All of a sudden, the whine of the generator got louder. They looked at one another in alarm. The ventilator fans hesitated.

Slowly, Sophie raised both hands in front of her and crossed all her fingers for luck. Solemnly, Sébastien did the same. They crossed their arms. They crossed their legs. They crossed their eyes and it wasn't even funny. The generator could NOT break down. It just couldn't.

But it did. The whine reached a feverish peak then went silent. The fans stopped turning. The milking machine ground to a halt. With the suction gone, the machines dropped away from the cows' udders. The cows began to bawl, confused.

This couldn't be happening. Sophie was paralyzed for almost a whole minute. When she could move, she grabbed Sébastien's hand and raced for the house shouting, "Papa! Maman!" at the top of her lungs.

But there was nothing to be done, nothing at all. Papa tinkered with the generator for a while and determined that a part deep inside the mechanism had broken.

"Overuse, probably," he said. "Nothing we can do."

"But our cows!" cried Sophie.

Papa pulled the truck keys out of his pocket. "I'll

go into town and see if anybody's got the part, or anything even close to the part that I can cobble up. And I'll register with the army for a new generator. I heard they're flying in generators from all across the country to help us. Evie, Sophie, see if you can finish milking this lot by hand. Take note of which ones got milked and which ones didn't. We can't possibly do them all by hand!" he added, shaking his head. "Sébastien, call the others and tell them what's happened. Tell them I'm trying my best to get another generator but they should try to make their own arrangements as well."

"But Papa," said Sébastien in a very small voice. "The phones are out too."

Papa put his face in his hands. *"Mon dieu!* Can anything else go wrong? I will drive to the other farms on my way home and tell them myself." He turned to go.

"Henri," Maman touched him on the shoulder. "Remember, the truck is almost out of gas." They were all four silent, standing around the carcass of the generator.

"Get the hand pump," Papa said finally, to no one in particular.

After Papa finished hand pumping more gas into the truck, he got into the cab without another word and drove away. The rest of the family stood out in the freezing rain and watched him go. This storm wasn't fun any more, not one bit.

DAY SIX
Saturday, January 10, 1998

THE SHELTER

ALICE SPENT ANOTHER ALMOST SLEEPLESS NIGHT. Almost, because she reckoned she must have dozed off at some point in the wee hours or she wouldn't be feeling as groggy as she was. Even though this shelter was better than the last one, all night there were still hundreds of people talking, going to the bathroom, moaning, crying, snoring and all kinds of other things that most people do in private. Alice was pretty sure that given a choice she'd pick loneliness over the chaos she was enduring now. Mrs. Hartley didn't agree. She'd made friends with the nurse and some of the volunteers and one of the ladies who had a cot near her. She was a lot less cranky when she had somebody to talk to, that was for sure. As Alice wiped the sleep from her eyes, she wondered what would happen today. It felt so strange to have absolutely no power over what was going to happen next.

Maybe she could read to the kids again. Yesterday, it had been fun while it lasted. But after an hour, most of the kids got tired of listening. They started to poke each other and act silly. Alice had to stop being a librarian and return the books to the bookstore. After that, the only thing to do was sit. Sit and stare. Sit and listen to all the fighting and the laughing and the arguing and the crying. Some of the grown-ups tried to organize games for the kids to play but the kids all said the games were lame. It was almost as if they had forgotten how to play any games that didn't include a video screen. So they just ran around and got into trouble, fighting over what program to watch on television. Alice sat and got frustrated. She had never felt so lonely in her life.

Breakfast was a weird combination of food. For dinner the soldiers trucked in food cooked at the big hospital kitchens. That was okay. But the other meals had a little bit of about a million different things. Lots of people were bringing the contents of their freezers to share around when they came to the shelter, rather than leave it at home to spoil. This morning, the menu consisted of scrambled eggs, sausage links, tuna casserole, lasagne, cabbage rolls, fish sticks and frozen peas. The volunteers were trying to heat stuff up in the tiny lunchrooms on each floor of the office tower, but that meant mostly everything was microwaved. Alice wished St-Viateur would show up with bagels, but they didn't. After breakfast, Alice helped Mrs. Hartley back to her bed. The old lady was more comfortable getting around with the cane that had been found for her, but the nurse wanted her to stay off her leg as much as possible. Alice plunked down on the end of her bed for the morning news update. Not only was it interesting, it was the one time of day that almost everybody in the shelter kept quiet.

Canada's second largest city is in serious trouble! intoned the TV announcer dramatically. *Millions of people are struggling in the freezing darkness!*

The good news: the rain has stopped for the time being and some areas will see sunshine today. The bad news: a cold front is coming and temperatures are expected to drop below minus ten overnight with winds gusting to forty kilometres per hour. This will hurt Hydro workers' efforts to repair downed lines, as the cold temperatures will force them to clear ice from lines by hand rather than machine to prevent further damage. Not to mention the increased discomfort they will suffer from spending long hours outside.

Alice bit her lip. Her poor dad.

Here's where we are today: there are now eleven dead

from carbon monoxide poisoning, hypothermia and falling ice. In addition to the three million previously without power, tens of thousands more in the Maritimes are now also in the dark. Montréal's two main pumping stations have lost power, so parts of the city have run out of water. If you have water, please boil it before using from now on to prevent disease. Emergency shelters are running out of beds and supplies, so if you have to go to a shelter bring your own sleeping bags and lawn chairs.

An ice jam in the St. François River has caused flooding in St. Nicéphore. Two hundred people had to be evacuated. The Ministry of Natural Resources has a plan to fly in chainsaws and the Federal Defense Department is setting up a winter tent camp in Vankleek Hill for a thousand hydro workers while they work on the downed lines. VIA Rail workers are walking along the rail lines, trying to clear debris and ice from the tracks.

Dramatic stories are pouring in from all over the disaster zone. One man, who was driving along Highway 20, had this to say, "I saw a pylon in front of me twist like it was plastic. It twisted in two, and then became a ball, and crumbled. The lines were all over the highway. After the first one fell, three others behind it collapsed. It was pretty scary."

Hydro-Québec is no longer talking about repairing the system. They will have to build it all over again.

The Premier of Québec has just called the United States to ask for a loan of beds and generators. "The situation has aggravated," he said. "I would ask Québecers to keep showing their solidarity and capacity to endure these trials." But out in the icy cold, Québecers are getting angry. People are asking why Hydro-Québec insisted everybody switch to electric heating. "If I'd kept my natural gas, I wouldn't be in this mess," said one man. "Like idiots, we did what we were told. Now look at us." On a lighter note, some people are complaining about not enough ice. When power was lost at indoor skating arenas throughout the disaster zone, ice-making equipment quit. The rinks have all melted.

Alice didn't know whether to laugh or cry when she heard that one. Mrs. Hartley wouldn't let it pass.

"How does that make you feel, Alice girl?" she asked. "Happy? Sad? Relieved?"

Why, oh why, did she always ask the hard questions? The old lady was worse than Aunt Evie for extracting the truth. This was none of her business.

"Don't glare at me, girl," said Mrs. Hartley fiercely. "I don't need to know the answer, but you do. Think about it."

Alice sat motionless on the end of the bed. "Relieved," she finally admitted, slumping her shoulders. "There, I said what you wanted me to say."

"Believe me, girl, I don't care what you say. Now go away and leave me in peace." With that, Mrs. Hartley turned on her side to take a nap.

Oh, how that old lady made her mad! Having a few friends to talk to hadn't made Mrs. Hartley less cranky at all.

Alice left in a huff. There were other things to think about right now. Maybe if she found Jean-Michel he'd let her borrow the keys to the bookstore again. But before she found him, another volunteer tapped her on the shoulder.

"Hello, dear, what's your name?" Alice told her.

"We've just been told that the bakery next door has been given a delivery of staples by the army: flour, sugar, eggs and things like that. They're looking for volunteers to make muffins to distribute to the shelters. Would you like to help?"

Would she? Alice was excited. She had never been inside a commercial bakery before. It was huge. The ovens and the fridges and the mixers were ten times the size of the ones they had at home and all the counters were sparkling stainless steel. She looked around in awe. And she wasn't the only one; there were a least a dozen kids her age volunteering, looking just as overwhelmed as she felt. The owner of the bakery was quite a jolly man, inviting all the volunteers to "Come in, come in!" The other bakers didn't look so welcoming. Maybe they thought the kids would have a food fight or break the machines or something. Alice stuck close to the owner. He was funny.

Monsieur le Muffin (surely that wasn't his real name?) split the kids into two groups, one to make muffins and one to make cookies. Cookies sounded like fun, but Monsieur le Muffin was taking the muffin group, so Alice stayed with him. They all got big white aprons and hats. For a moment, Alice thought about Sébastien and his new video camera. He'd go nuts if he could film this! While the real bakers started up the ovens and the mixers, some of the kids were given instructions for measuring, some got started preparing the baking tins, and Alice and three other kids were taken into the pantry to choose ingredients to put into the muffins. The pantry was another incredible hidden kingdom, as far as Alice was concerned. Container after container of nuts, raisins, chocolate chips, dried fruit, sprinkles, sesame seeds, coconut, maple sugar and a whole bunch of other things Alice couldn't even name.

The baker gave them each a stainless steel bowl. "Fill each one with something different that would taste good in a muffin," shouted Monsieur le Muffin. "Be creative! Be inspired! Our muffins must lift the spirit and spread happiness!"

Alice couldn't help but laugh. That was a tall order for even the very best muffin. Alice headed for the maple sugar, her favourite. The other three went for the chocolate chips.

"Who are you?" asked a blonde girl.

"Alice."

"Rachel."

"Tucker."

" Hi. I'm Saskia. My house burned down."

The other three looked at Saskia in shock. "You're kidding!" said Rachel.

"Nope. Right to the ground. Kept us warm for a while."

"That's awful," said Alice.

"It's so cool," said Tucker. "How high were the flames?"

The girls just looked at him. "Boys!" they said in unison. He just shrugged.

After the four of them filled their bowls, they went back to the main kitchen to wait for the muffin batter to be ready. Tucker stared at the bowls. "That baker guy said to be creative. Why don't we mix things up a little?"

Rachel looked at their ingredients critically. "What if we mixed the walnuts and the raisins?"

"Yeah, and the pecans and the maple sugar?" Alice got into the swing of it.

"What goes with coconut?" asked Saskia, heading back into the pantry. They found more bowls and began to combine their finds. From time to time, Monsieur le Muffin wandered by, smiling indulgently. He even gave some suggestions. By the time the batter was ready, so were their creations, bowl after bowl of concoctions that were more or less palatable. One of the other bakers raised his eyebrows when he saw what was in the bowls.

"Interesting," he said to the four of them drily. "Let's hope that whoever eats one of these muffins remembered their toothbrush. With that much sugar, their teeth will rot out before morning." The girls giggled, while Tucker simply looked lofty. As they waited for the muffins to bake, they compared notes. Saskia's house burned down because they'd lit a fire in the fireplace without realizing that it was all clogged up with soot. She wasn't too worried about it, though.

"Normally I would be," she said in a matter-of-fact way. "But this isn't normal. Nothing is normal. Dad says we all got out alive, so it could have been worse. And he's right."

Wow. Alice wondered how it was possible to shut worries off like that. She wished she could do it. Where would Saskia's family go when they left the shelter? "Why do you have that note?" asked Alice curiously. Saskia looked down at the paper pinned to her shirt that read "Danish."

"Oh, lots of us kids have them," Saskia replied in an offhand way. "It means we speak another language and can translate for some of the old folks who can't speak English or French. There are a lot of new immigrants in the shelters, and they're pretty scared."

Alice was impressed. She could barely speak two languages, much less three.

Rachel's story was similar to Alice's. Her mom was a nurse and living at the hospital because there were so many patients to look after. So the soldiers came to get Rachel just like they had Alice. It made Alice feel like she had a buddy. It was a cool feeling. She and Rachel smiled at one another.

Tucker was at the shelter with his mom, his dad, his five brothers and sisters, two dogs, three cats, a goldfish and his mom's favourite houseplant. "I love it here," he stated with a straight face. "It's so quiet and calm compared to my house." The girls just couldn't help but laugh at his jokes.

In twenty minutes time, the muffins were baked. A dozen tall white hats peered into the ovens to catch a first glimpse of their creations. Just then, there was a commotion outside. Tucker ran to the window of the bakery.

"*Qu'est-ce que c'est?*" demanded Monsieur le Muffin. "Who interrupts the creation?"

"I can't see," said Tucker. "There's a whole bunch of people out on the street. Wait – they're waving. And shouting. I don't know, but it looks like, well, it looks kind of like a parade. That can't be right, can it?"

Curious, the rest of the bakers joined Tucker at the window. They all strained to see. Alice was the first to understand.

"It's the Americans!" she cried. "The Americans

have come to help us! And she was right. A line of great big hydro trucks was inching along the icy street. They had enormous American flags tied to the front grills. The linemen inside were smiling and waving. Soldiers, police officers, volunteers from the shelters, the few passersby – all of them clapped and cheered as the trucks went by. Help had come.

Just seeing them made Alice feel hopeful, which gave her an idea. Rushing over to the cooling racks, Alice loaded a plate with hot muffins and cookies.

"May I?" she asked Monsieur le Muffin. The jolly baker nodded with a smile. Alice ran outside, coatless, hatless and bootless, but she didn't care. The ice slowed her down a bit, but she still managed to pick her way to a truck. Reaching as high as she could, she offered the warm treats.

"Thank you, thank you!" she cried. "My dad is out there. He's a lineman too. Thank you for coming to help him!"

"Wal, little lady, ain't no trouble a'tall," drawled one of the linemen. "It's the neighbourly thing to do, wouldn't ya say? But I ain't sure we got ourselves enough clothes for this here weather ya got going on."

"How cold is it, anyway?" Alice laughed.

"Where are you from?" she asked, as she followed along beside the truck.

"We hail from Raleigh, North Carolina, miss," replied the lineman.

"Well, if you need extra clothes, you talk to my dad. He'll get you some," said Alice solicitously. "The army will too. Don't catch cold."

The lineman smiled as he handed the empty plate back to her. "I'll make sure I do, little lady," he said with a grin. "Now you get back inside and keep warm too."

Alice took the plate. As the truck moved off, tears gathered in her eyes. They'd come over a thousand kilometres to help, in weather more wicked than they had probably ever seen. But still they came. Alice didn't need a coat, she felt so warm inside.

Now that the trucks had passed, the bakery volunteers were busy packing up the goodies for the various shelters nearby. Alice pitched in, and in no time the boxes were ready for pickup. When the cleaning up was finished, they all thanked Monsieur le Muffin, who answered with a courtly bow, not too low because of his portly shape.

"My pleasure, *mes petits, merci beaucoup, merci, merci!* We must have treats in a crisis, it is *très important!*" Rachel and Alice looked at one another and burst out laughing. Now that was a strategy – treats in a crisis. With all the worries everybody had right now, that would be a lot of treats!

The group of volunteers had just made it back to the shelter when there was another commotion. Once again, Tucker saw it first. "It's the Montréal Canadiens!" he exclaimed. "They're here!" Tucker was off like a shot.

Saskia stood on her tiptoes. "Just looks like a bunch of guys signing autographs to me."

"Like hockey players are important or something," Rachel added.

"Well, it's not like they have anything else to do," went on Alice. "Their ice rinks have melted."

All three girls laughed as they marched off in the opposite direction with their noses in the air. They split up to check on their families after agreeing to meet for supper. Alice hugged herself a little as she made her way to Mrs. Hartley's corner. She couldn't wait to tell the old lady about the new friends she'd made, and about the muffins and the American linemen.

But when Alice arrived at Mrs. Hartley's cot, it was clear they'd be doing no talking. Mrs. Hartley was curled up in a ball, shivering so hard Alice was afraid her false teeth would fall out. Her lips were blue and her crablike hands were convulsively clutching at the sleeping bag. She looked to be in terrible pain.

"Mrs. Hartley, what's wrong?" cried Alice. "Do you need your insulin?" Mrs. Hartley shook her head. She could barely talk.

"My nitro," she gasped. "Under the bed."

Alice didn't know what nitro was. She thought it was something people used to make bombs. Surely that wasn't what Mrs. Hartley meant. It must be some kind of pill or something. Alice dug out Mrs. Hartley's overnight bag from under the bed and unzipped it. She sat back on her heels in dismay. There were no pills in it. Not a single bottle. But Mrs. Hartley had arrived with at least a dozen bottles of medicine, Alice was sure. Where were they?

Mrs. Hartley was shaking even harder. Alice had to do something.

She stood up and looked at Mrs. Hartley's new friend in the next bed. Maybe she would know. But that lady was asleep. She looked at the bed on the other side. In it sat a diminutive Asian woman, a woman older than anybody Alice had ever seen before. But age hadn't affected her energy. The tiny woman was staring straight at Alice, pointing to Mrs. Hartley, pointing to the overnight bag, pointing to the door, gesturing this way and that, while the whole time letting loose an agitated stream of a language Alice had never heard before. This woman knew something. Alice thought of Saskia's note. She needed to find a kid who could speak whatever language this woman spoke and she needed to find the nurse. Alice put her finger up to the tiny woman, trying to make her understand that she was going to get help. Then she ran.

She couldn't find a nurse or doctor anywhere. Just great. She found a knot of kids and scanned their shirts. One girl had a note that said "Chinese." Alice grabbed her by the arm and towed the bewildered girl back to Mrs. Hartley.

Alice pointed to the woman. "Can you tell me what she's saying?"

"Nope," said the girl. "I only speak Chinese. That's Korean." The girl left.

Alice ran back to the kids' area. "Anybody here speak Korean?" she shouted over the din. "It's an emergency!"

A little girl who couldn't have been more than six was pushed through the crowd. Obediently she followed Alice, who was still casting her eyes about for a doctor or a nurse. Nothing. No one. Nada. When they got to the old people's area, the little girl went straight to the tiny woman and listened. Then she turned to Alice.

"The grandmother says that big boys came. They looked in all the bags and took all the pills. No pills left for anybody. They took them all. She yell but they laugh. Nobody stop them."

"Ask her to describe the big boys," said Alice urgently. The tiny woman let loose another torrent of words. The little girl didn't understand all of them, but she gave Alice a pretty good picture all the same.

"Where did they go?" The little girl asked the question. The tiny woman pointed in agitated fashion. Alice turned to run in the direction she pointed but at the last minute remembered her manners.

"Please tell her thanks," she told the girl. "You too. I'll try to get the pills back."

For the first time, the little girl looked scared.

"Don't!" she said urgently. "Those boys are bad boys. They'll hurt you!"

"I won't let them," replied Alice fiercely. She took a last look at Mrs. Hartley and ran. This was unbelievable. Sure, she'd heard about gangs, but this was absolutely too ridiculous for words. She had never been so furious. Mrs. Hartley might die, just because she didn't have a pill worth a couple of bucks?

Of course, as soon as Alice left the room she felt stupid. As if she could take on a bunch of thieves. But she had to get help somehow. Where were the grown-ups when you needed them?

Alice ran to the area that had been set up as a registration desk. Quickly she explained the problem to the young man at the desk, who stood up in dismay.

"The Director's gone to a meeting with the mayor," the young man blurted out. "I'm just a volunteer."

"We have to find *somebody* to help!" Alice replied. She ran into the main TV room. Looking around, she picked out a guy who was big and muscular, the kind of guy that looked a little scary. He had a snake tattoo circling his neck. He listened to her story, frowned, and collected a couple of other men.

"Wait here," he said firmly to Alice and the young man from the desk.

The "bad boys" hadn't even tried to hide their booty. The men found them easily, holed up in one of the offices down the hall. In no time, the tattooed guy was back. He handed Alice a big plastic bag filled with pill bottles.

"Thanks!"

"No trouble," grinned the man. "We got it covered."

Alice ran back to Mrs. Hartley and dropped to her knees beside her cot. She dumped out the bottles and frantically looked for something called nitro. Mrs. Hartley had stopped shaking, but she was pale, almost blue, and too quiet. Alice found one. The bottle said nitro but it was for somebody else. Would it still work? Alice knew that you weren't supposed to take somebody else's medicine. What if she killed Mrs. Hartley?

Just then the nurse rushed in. "They told me you were looking for me. What's happened?" She looked at all the bottles in surprise. "Where did you get all these?" she asked suspiciously.

"Long story," said Alice. "Tell you later. Mrs. Hartley said she needed nitro. I can't find hers. Will this work?"

The nurse nodded and helped Mrs. Hartley get a pill under her tongue. In no time she began to relax. Murmuring, "Thank you," Mrs. Hartley fell asleep.

"Explain!" demanded the nurse. Alice explained.

When the Director returned, the little Korean girl was asked to translate the grandmother's story once again. The Director shook his head in dismay. "It's to be expected," he said sadly.

Expected? Expected! Alice was outraged; she

couldn't believe her ears. She felt a little better when she heard the Director use his walkie-talkie to call building security. With the help of the tattooed man and his friends, they rounded up the boys and kept them in an office. Security called the police and the whole group was expelled from the shelter.

"You can't do this!" they shouted when the police came to take them away. "We'll freeze! We're underage. You have to let us stay!"

"Don't worry, you won't be outside," replied one of the police officers sternly. "But you can be sure you won't be in a place as nice as this." The police escorted them out. Alice could hardly imagine a place worse than where they were. It made her feel a little bad for the boys, but not much.

Alice took up a post beside Mrs. Hartley's bed. The nurse said that she'd been suffering from something called angina. It was like heart pain. The nitro helped, but Mrs. Hartley wouldn't have died. It didn't matter, thought Alice. Something else might happen. Alice reached up and gently patted Mrs. Hartley's hand, smiling when she felt the newly trimmed fingernails. As Alice lay on her foamie beside the cot, her mind was racing. How could some people travel a thousand kilometres to help and others steal medicine from old people? How could people like her dad work sixteen-hour shifts in freezing rain and frigid temperatures to get power back on for all the people, and others take generators just for themselves?

Then something else *did* happen. One of the policemen came back. He had a grim look on his face as he looked around for the Director. Keeping an eye on Mrs. Hartley, Alice sidled over to where the Director and the policeman were talking, keeping out of sight behind a potted plant. What was going on?

"Monsieur le Directeur," said the policeman quietly. "Begin making plans to move all these people. We may have to evacuate the entire city."

Alice's eyes widened with fear.

DAY SIX
Saturday, January 10, 1998

THE FARM

S OPHIE DIDN'T WANT TO GET OUT OF BED. IT wasn't the cold. She was so used to being cold now that her bedroom almost felt warm. And the kitchen, with the toasty wood stove, would be practically hot. And she'd have hot food to eat, which was more than most families in the Triangle of Darkness could boast. Everything about her life was just fine. Except that her cows were dying and Sophie didn't know how she could bear it.

The first two died while Papa was in town, trying to get another generator or at least a replacement part. Maman said it was pneumonia. She had to get the front-end loader and hoist each carcass up, then take them one by one down to the lower meadow. She dumped them there to freeze, until they were able to take care of the carcasses properly. Sébastien wanted to have a funeral. Maman said no. She said it was just the beginning. More cows were going to die and there would be too many funerals. That made him cry. It made them all cry. Maman made them hot drinks but this was too big a problem to be solved by *chocolat chaud*.

When Papa heard, he went very still.

The news from Saint-Hyacinthe was terrible. Papa told Sébastien not to worry that the phones were out. There was no point in trying to chase the milk trucks because now the milk processing plants were shut down too. There weren't enough generators to keep them going. All their milk would have to be dumped. Assuming they could do any milking at all. Papa had registered for a generator, but he was Number 62 on the list.

They all four had gone to the barn to try to finish the milking that had been cut short. The whole family worked for hours, each taking a cow, hand milking just enough to take the pressure off the udder. It made the cows a little more comfortable, but then what? It took a half an hour to fully milk a cow and with fifty of them, well, forty-eight now, there simply were not enough hours in the day to get it done. Not to mention that their hands couldn't take the strain. Hand-milking was hard work, especially with cows who weren't used to it.

Even under the covers Sophie could hear the cows, her girls, bawling in distress. It was a horrible noise. They were thirsty and uncomfortable. Their lives had been totally disrupted and they didn't know why. And what could she do except watch them suffer? There was simply no point in getting up. There was no solution. She would rather pull the covers over her head than hear them cry out their agony and watch them die one by one.

"SOPHIE! ARE YOU AWAKE?" shouted Maman. Sophie groaned. "Come down for breakfast. We have work to do!"

Sophie dragged herself out of bed and headed unwillingly to the kitchen. Sébastien was already sitting in front of a tower of pancakes.

"*Petit cochon,*" spat Sophie, more out of habit than anything else. Sébastien, as usual, ignored her. Sophie scraped her chair noisily across the wooden floor, rattled the dishes on the table as she sat down heavily, then turned a belligerent face towards Maman. Sophie wanted to make sure that everybody knew she was upset.

Maman turned from the sink and put her hands on her hips. "*Ma fille,* being miserable with us won't help anything. We didn't bring the storm."

Sophie scowled. Maybe so, but she sure didn't feel like being all polite and smiley. She needed some way to show how upset she was, some way to show the world that this just wasn't *fair*! There didn't seem to be anything she could do except be miserable, so she was just going to go ahead and *be* miserable.

Maman was still staring at her, eyebrows raised, hands on hips. Sophie shifted a little in her chair. Maman kept staring. Sophie began to feel uncomfortable. Finally she said angrily, "If I can't feel miserable, how am I supposed to feel? Happy? Thrilled? Excited?" she added sarcastically. "Aren't I allowed to feel the way I want to feel?"

Maman sighed. "Of course you can," she replied. "But you shouldn't inflict your feelings on others, not if it doesn't help anything. Making everybody feel worse doesn't help. So can you allow us all to move on?"

"Move on to what?" Sophie said under her breath, as she turned to get a breakfast plate.

"Say that out loud," commanded Maman. "For once, Sophie, let it out. Reach down inside and say what you mean, get it out in the open, deal with it. Stop keeping the stuff that hurts you inside!"

Sophie was shocked. She and Maman had never really argued before, not like this. It was way easier to pretend that they weren't fighting even when they were. They would sigh at one another, roll their eyes and walk away, always pretending on the surface that nothing was wrong. They never said the words out loud. Sébastien had stopped eating with a forkful of pancakes halfway to his mouth, maple syrup dripping everywhere. The only sound in the kitchen was the crackling of the wood stove.

Sophie couldn't say a word.

Finally Maman shook her head sadly. With a crooked grin, she said, "Sophie, when you were little, you had the most terrible temper tantrums. You would throw yourself to the ground and beat your little fists and scream and yell whenever you didn't get your way. Papa and I taught you to stop. Now, I think we taught you too well. Now you can't let your feelings out at all. I think you need to have a tantrum. God knows this storm is worth a really good one." Wearily, Maman turned back to the dishes in the sink.

Sophie could feel her eyes filling up with tears. Maman had never spoken to her like that before. Sophie felt hurt, and ashamed. She wanted to hold her ground, to continue to punish them because they weren't as sad as she was. She wanted to fight back. But a little voice in her head was telling her Maman was right. Everybody was sad, but it was only Sophie who wanted to hide in her bed.

She held herself very, very still. She couldn't *inflict* herself on them. Maman had said so. Sophie didn't think she could hold the tears in for long and she knew she had to, because if she started to cry she'd never stop. At first, she just wanted to get away. Then she thought of Mélisande. The calf wouldn't yell at her.

Sophie grabbed her coat from the peg in the kitchen and ran to the barn. She curled up beside Mélisande, wrapping her arms around the calf's warm neck. This was good. But everything else was so bad.

Sophie didn't know how long she'd been in Mélisande's pen when she heard the commotion in the lane. Somebody — or something — was coming. Sophie held herself even tighter. She wanted to see. She wanted to help if she could, but now she was embarrassed. She didn't want to *inflict* herself on anybody. Sophie knew she was being stupid. The longer she stayed hidden the harder it would be to face everybody.

Sophie stood up and looked down the lane. There were a couple of army trucks in the yard. But there was no trailer, so they hadn't brought a generator. Why had they come? As Sophie watched, eight men, strangers, got out of the trucks. Sophie stepped a little closer to get a better view. They looked like farmers, but like no farmers she'd ever seen before. They wore very plain clothes and big black hats. Sophie's curiosity finally overrode her embarrassment and she went outside to find out what was going on.

Papa was shaking hands with the strangers. When Sophie arrived, Papa introduced her. The men smiled at her. They looked very kind. Who were they?

"Sophie, Sébastien, run to the barn and get the

cows who are most uncomfortable."

"Should we take them to the milking parlour?" asked Sophie.

"No, get them over to the maternity pen as fast as you can." Sophie and Sébastien looked at one another in surprise and took off at a run.

The barn was a terrible place. The noise the frightened cows made hurt Sophie's heart. How to choose who was most uncomfortable?

"Sébastien," she called urgently. "The prime milkers. Get them — they'll have the fullest udders." Sébastien understood immediately. Not all cows produced the same amount of milk. The ones that produced the most would be in the most pain. Picking a few cows nearly created a stampede for the milking parlour. All the cows wanted to go there. Sophie tried to calm them as best she could, even though she had to yell to be heard over all the bawling. Once out of the barn, she and Sébastien had to force the selected cows away from the milking parlour and over to the maternity pen.

The strangers were washing their hands. Each had a small, old-fashioned milking stool and a pail. Frowning, Sophie began the process of hosing down the cows and cleaning their teats. Surely they weren't going to try to hand-milk the cows, were they? There were too many!

But that is exactly what the strangers did. When

the cows were ready, the strangers sat down on their little stools and began to milk. Now Sophie understood why they couldn't use the milking parlour. There, people worked in the pit so the cows' udders were at the right height. The cows would have been too high for the hand-milkers to reach.

Sophie watched the strangers work in awe. She had never seen anything like it. Their hands were big and strong. With every squeeze they were able to get more milk out of the teat than she could with ten squeezes. They finished a cow almost as fast as the milking machine could. Sophie, Sébastien and Papa kept busy leading cows back and forth from the maternity pen and cleaning them for milking. The soldiers kept busy taking the full pails and dumping the milk in a ditch away from the barn. Maman kept busy making hot drinks and insisting the strangers rest and eat every so often. It was like an assembly line. Sophie felt like she was part of something very important. For the second time that day she felt tears come to her eyes. This storm was making her feel so happy and so sad, all at the same time, that her head was whirling.

Hours later, the bawling stopped. The cows were milked. Every last one. The strangers' hands had never cramped, never frozen in place. They were magical. As the men loaded their tiny stools back into the army trucks, the whole family stood side by side to thank them.

"No need," said the strangers quietly. "We are all farmers. We all care for our animals the best way we can. And if our neighbour needs help, it is our duty and our pleasure. Godspeed."

The army drove the strangers away, but none of the four of them moved out of the wind. It blew all around but didn't seem to touch them. It was as if the strangers had left a protective arm around them.

"Who *were* they?" asked Sébastien.

"Mennonites," said Papa. "They are dairy farmers just like us. They are also religious people and one of their beliefs is that they should depend on themselves, not on electricity. Not because electricity is bad, but because community is more important. And it is that sense of community that we just witnessed, even though they are from Ontario and we live in Québec."

Sébastien thought about that. "If we didn't depend on electricity, we wouldn't be in so much trouble," he mused.

Papa looked at him. "Nor would we have all the things that we have. It's a tricky problem, isn't it?"

They went inside for a snack and a warm-up. Papa had a short nap. Sophie tried to read a book. Sébastien played with his video camera, taking shots of icicles through a window. All of a sudden, the phone rang. It seemed such a strange and alien sound that no one thought to pick it up.

"Phone!" shouted Sophie, finally, as she came to

her senses. She ran to get it.

"Allo, bonjour?"

"Sophie, it's Uncle Pete. How are you all doing?" It was Alice's dad!

With a big grin, Sophie told him all the news, about the generator and the neighbours and Sébastien's schedule and the Mennonites.

"Wow," chuckled Uncle Pete. "You have certainly been having some exciting times! I have too, although I've been so busy that I haven't even had a chance to go home. I'm sleeping in a tent, can you believe it? Right now I'm at the Hydro office, though, so I'm finally able to charge my cell. Now, may I speak to Alice, please? I miss my little girl!"

Sophie's smile faded. "No, Uncle Pete, you can't," she said seriously. "Alice isn't here." Maman looked up sharply and went to wake Papa.

"What?! I thought your papa was going to pick her up and bring her to the farm! What happened?" he said anxiously.

Papa came hurrying into the room, holding his hand out for the phone. Sophie handed it to him, eyes wide. Quickly, Papa explained how close he'd come and about the bridges being closed. "Our phones were out by the time I got back to the farm," he said. "I don't know where I could have reached you anyway. Don't worry, Pierre, Alice is smart. She will know what to do, how to look after herself."

The two fathers talked a little longer, and then Papa hung up the phone. "I told him to go home," he said. "Alice will either be there, or she will have left a note." They were all quiet. Alice and Uncle Pete were their family.

Finally Maman spoke. "I thought that Pierre would have known the bridges were closed, that we couldn't get her. I thought he would have gone home by now."

Papa nodded his head. "I thought so too. And he thought we had picked her up before the bridges closed. He was sure she was with us so he didn't go home. *C'est terrible!*"

Sophie was horrified. They had all believed that Uncle Pete was home with Alice. Quickly she dialed Alice's number, just in case. The phone rang and rang and rang. What did that mean? Was her phone not working, or was Alice not there to pick up? If she wasn't there, where *was* she?

After that, none of them could sit still. Papa decided to go into town to get a news update and ask again about a generator. Maman took one look at Sophie and Sébastien and waved them off. "Go, go, *allez avec papa,*" she said. "I'll mind the animals."

In no time, Sophie, Sébastien and Papa were driving slowly along the concession road that led to town. The roads were awful; much worse than Tuesday when Maman had taken them to school. Had that been only four days ago? It seemed like a year. Since Tuesday, their whole world had changed. Papa drove straight to the Town Hall. It was the centre for all information and collection of supplies. Striding into the hall, Papa headed directly for a cluster of farmers he knew.

"*Bonjour, bonjour,* Henri," they said. "*Comment ça va?*" The men exchanged stories. The pig and poultry farmers were badly off. Many pigs and chickens had been lost. The dairymen were desperate. Tens of thousands of animals' lives were at stake, not to mention the lost milk. And it wasn't just the milk that was being poured into ditches and drains all over the region that was lost. Cows that weren't milked went dry. They would stop producing milk until they gave birth to another calf, and that took nine months. What would happen to the milk supply until then?

Sophie crept close to the knot of men, listening to all they said. Sébastien backed away, filming the animated discussion from a distance with his ever-present camera. Sophie wondered what kind of a movie her brother was going to make with all this footage. A disaster flick? A story about the end of the world? Sophie bent her ear to listen some more. The farmers' organization, the *Association des Producteurs Agricoles,* was in charge of finding and distributing generators. There were still many farms in need. Sophie saw Papa frown. When would they get theirs?

The Red Cross was in town, helping out at the shelter. That surprised Sophie. She hadn't known that Saint-Hyacinthe had a shelter. Didn't everybody have a wood stove to keep them warm?

"There are two thousand people at the shelter," said M. Champlain. "It's over at the high school, the *Polyvalente Hyacinthe Delorme*. They say the lineup for the shower is more than two hundred people long!"

Another man jumped in. "The police are going door to door, forcing people from their homes. They say many would rather freeze than leave. The Prime Minister of Canada even went on the television to encourage people to go to the shelters. He said that people are more important than belongings, and staying safe is most important. *'Your community stands ready to make you safe and warm.'* That's what he said. But who wants to go to those places?"

All the men began to speak at once. Sophie felt so confused. She thought about the Mennonites. Their community was standing ready. Hers didn't seem to be doing as good a job.

Papa spent some time negotiating with other farmers about the loan of a generator. But everyone was struggling. No one had any generator time to loan. Someone turned up a radio, and the Town Hall quieted to listen.

There are now 7,500 troops working in the disaster zone, the largest peacetime deployment on home soil

*in history. A hundred thousand people are now living
in shelters. Damage estimates are in the billions of
dollars. Water and sewage is failing in a dozen communities. It may be weeks before power is back on.
And now the weather report: the freezing rain has
stopped. But tomorrow's forecast is minus fifteen
degrees. Those who are cold will get much colder
before power is restored.*

No one in the Town Hall spoke. What was there to
say? Papa motioned to Sophie and Sébastien and they
followed him out to the truck. There was nothing for
them in town except bad news. Papa turned the truck
towards home and Maman.

Six more cows had died. Sébastien ran to his room
and Papa pounded the kitchen table in anger. Sophie
did nothing. She couldn't let herself feel anything or
she would feel too much. Maman had dumped the
carcasses in the lower meadow. The rest of the herd
was beginning to bawl. It had been hours since the
Mennonites had milked them and their udders were
filling once again. There was no generator on the way,
and without the team of hand-milkers there was so
little they could do. Sophie wanted to get as far away
from the distress in the barn as she could. She decided
to walk to the sugar bush.

The family sugar bush was one of Sophie's
favourite places. She loved to visit it in summer, when

she would take a book and read in the shade of the beautiful maple trees. She loved to visit it in autumn when the maple leaves turned fiery crimson. She particularly loved to visit it in spring when the sap started to run in the trees. The whole family worked together to collect the sap and make it into maple syrup. They loaded up their gear on a sled that Papa's grandfather had made: a drill, a hammer, spiles, hooks, buckets, and lids.

Once in the bush, Papa selected the trees for tapping. Then he picked a spot on each tree about three feet from the ground, over a large root or under a big branch where the sap was running. He drilled a little hole. Sophie got to tap the spiles into the hole. The spile was like a tube that let the sap run out of the tree. Sébastien always called it a tap and it was sort of like that, except you couldn't turn it off and on. Then Sébastien put a little hook on the spile and hung a bucket from the hook to collect the dripping sap. The buckets had special lids to keep the sap clean.

Every day she and Sébastien would collect the sap and pour it into big containers that were dug into the snow beside their sugar shack. Then one special day when Maman determined they had collected enough sap, she would have Papa build the great outdoor fire that let them make maple syrup. Maman boiled the sap in a big flat pan over the fire. It took forty gallons of sap to make just one gallon of syrup, which meant

a lot of boiling. That's why they did the cooking outside. Maman said if they did it in the kitchen the wall-
paper would probably peel right off the walls from all
the steam.

Sophie liked maple syrup just as much as the next
person (which was a lot) but it wasn't her favourite
maple treat. Sometimes Maman made maple sugar
candy. To make that, Maman had to keep boiling the
sap past the syrup stage until it got really thick. At
exactly the right moment, Maman would take the pan
off the heat and start to beat it with a wooden spoon.
She would beat it and beat it until the colour got
lighter and lighter and the consistency got thicker and
thicker and she couldn't beat it any more. Then they
poured it out on waxed paper to cool. It was just like
fudge and so delicious it made Sophie's mouth water
just thinking about it. But sugar candy wasn't her
favourite maple treat either.

Sophie's absolutely most favourite maple treat was
sugar on snow. That's what her family called it anyway.
After Maman had boiled the sap to syrup and they had
poured it into bottles for storage, sometimes she
would leave a little syrup in the pan. She'd boil it a
little longer until it stuck to the spoon. Then, quick as
a wink, Maman would pick up the pan with her hot
mitts and pour the thick syrup onto a clean patch of
snow. It would melt into the snow, capturing tiny ice
crystals as it hardened. Quickly, Sophie and Sébastien

would take a stick or a spoon and wrap the thick, toffee-like candy around it before the syrup hardened completely. They'd stick it into their mouths where it would be hot and cold all at the same time, thick and sweet and filled with cold ice crystals. Sophie liked to put a big piece in her mouth and just leave it there to melt slowly, slowly down her throat. It was heaven. Sometimes she needed to eat a pickle after, it was so sweet, but it was worth it.

As she walked towards the sugar bush, Sophie thought about the way her family collected sap. Other people said their way was old-fashioned. Other people used tubes and lines and vacuum pressure to make the work easier. Sophie smiled to herself. This year, if the power was still out by the time the sap started to run, maybe they'd be the only ones who would be able to collect the sap, the only ones who didn't need electricity!

Sophie was still smiling to herself as she walked past the last equipment shed and turned towards the sugar bush. She stopped in horror. Her sugar bush was gone.

Where there had been tall, stately trees, now there was nothing but a pile of broken limbs. Some trees had split completely in half. Others were weighed down with so much ice that the tops of the trees touched the ground. They looked like giant ice cubes, not trees. And the rest had lost all their branches. The trees were over a hundred years old and not a single one was left untouched. The ice had completely destroyed the sugar bush, the bush that had given her family maple syrup for three generations.

Sophie could take no more. She tried to keep still, to hold it all in, to keep control. She closed her eyes and tried to stay calm. But she could feel herself start to crack up. She could feel her control breaking away like a glacier falling into the sea and all of a sudden she didn't care any more. Sophie ran to the broken branches and began to kick the ice off them. She kicked as hard as she could, she kicked until she lost her balance and fell into the snow. Then she threw the broken branches as far as she could. She stomped on them, breaking them into smaller and smaller pieces. Then she screamed. She screamed at the sky and she screamed at the ice and she screamed at all that was not fair. She screamed until she lost her voice and then she started to sob.

It was Maman who found her. Maman captured Sophie in her arms and held her tight until the sobbing turned into hiccups. "That was an excellent tantrum!" praised Maman. "And," she added sadly, looking around at the bent and broken trees, "you couldn't have found a better reason."

DAY SEVEN
Sunday, January 11, 1998

MAMAN HAD BEEN RIGHT. SOPHIE HAD TO admit that Maman was almost always right. Almost. The temper tantrum had made her feel better. The sadness wasn't gone. How could she not be sad when her cows were still dying? But the misery was. She'd been able to sleep the whole night through.

Now she could concentrate on action. She had to find Alice. The cows were important, keeping them alive was important, but Alice was more important. But Sophie didn't know where to start. She needed Sébastien.

After a quick breakfast, the whole family headed out to the barn. They took turns washing down the cows and hand milking, giving their hands a chance to rest by changing activities.

"Not too much, not too much," Papa kept shouting. "Five minutes each or we won't get them finished. Then we start again!" The milking strategy had been a difficult decision. Milk some of the cows completely to keep at least some healthy and producing, or milk all of the cows a little bit to ease their pain? Papa had decided to milk all the cows. He was willing to lose future milk production to help all of his cows be more comfortable. So round and round they went until their hand muscles froze up. Sophie was beginning to hate their expensive milking machines. If they hadn't depended on them, the herd wouldn't be as big and the family would be able to manage the hand milking. *Don't cry over spilt milk.* Maman's words kept coming back to Sophie. Well, they sure had a lot of spilt milk now, she thought, as she dumped yet another bucket of milk into the ditch.

When she and Sébastien ended up on side-by-side cows, Sophie asked him for help.

"How can we find Alice?"

"You're asking *me?*" Sébastien asked in disbelief.

"Well, you're good at strategies and planning and stuff. How do we find her?" Sophie blushed. It was probably the first time she'd ever praised her brother for something. No wonder he was confused.

"Well," said Sébastien thoughtfully, letting the moment pass, "Uncle Pete is going to phone us when he gets home. If she's there, it's all good. If not, we have to think about where she might go. Uncle Pete will probably check with the neighbours. Maybe she's at a shelter. That's where everybody's supposed to go, isn't it? And they probably make people register, so there'll be a list or something."

"But how do we find out where the shelters are? We don't have the Internet or anything," asked Sophie.

Sébastien thought for a minute. "Phone the Red Cross," he said finally. "They're running the Saint-Hyacinthe shelter. Maybe they're running all of them."

Sophie looked at her little brother strangely. "How did you get to be so smart?" she said, almost to herself.

"How did you get to be so nice?" retorted Sébastien. "You're weirding me out!"

Sophie had to smile.

ALICE WOKE UP CRAMPED AND STIFF. She honestly didn't think she could spend one more night in the shelter, Mrs. Hartley or no Mrs. Hartley. Last night had been the worst. All night long people kept arriving. The police were making people come because it was getting dangerous to stay in houses with no heat. And the absolutely worst part was that a lot of the people were sick. The nurse told her it was food poisoning. People were eating food that had spoiled and then they got sick and came to the shelter for help. Which was a good thing, reasoned Alice, except it was totally disgusting. Some of them didn't make it to the bathroom.

Alice took breakfast to Mrs. Hartley. The old lady was in good spirits this morning, but still tired and weak from yesterday's angina attack. After that, Alice didn't know what she would do. What would her adventure be today? Muffins? The bookstore? The roof caving in? Having lunch? Tying her shoelaces? It was bewildering not to know what was going to happen next and waiting for something to happen was boring, boring, boring.

She found Jean-Michel first. He had a big box of dollar store prizes. "What are you doing?" she asked. "Are we going to play Bingo or something?"

"Better!" said Jean-Michel. "We're playing *Lotto-Douche!*"

"A shower lottery?" asked Alice. "What on earth is that?"

"Well," Jean-Michel leaned towards her and whispered, "I don't mean to complain, but have you smelled this place?"

"I'm trying not to," retorted Alice, wrinkling her nose. "It's disgusting!"

"Yeah, well, it's a problem. There's not a lot of hot water and nobody likes cold showers and the stink factor is rising. So we're going to give prizes to people who shower!" Jean-Michel grinned, looking very proud of himself. He showed Alice a big box. "The owner of the dollar store in the mall donated the prizes. Aren't they great?"

Alice was skeptical. "You really think somebody will take a cold shower to win a..." she rooted through the box, "...hula skirt?"

Jean-Michel looked deflated. "I thought it would be fun," he said. "You don't think it will work?"

"Sure it will!" Alice said with a forced smile. Jeepers, she hadn't wanted to hurt his feelings or anything. "Everybody's bored. It'll be something to do. Go for it!"

Jean-Michel went off whistling. He was totally amazing, Alice decided. She had never met anybody so cheerful. As he left, Alice heard a commotion at the front desk. More arrivals. She groaned inwardly. She hoped they weren't sick. Alice sat down to watch *The Simpsons* on television in one of the office boardrooms. She'd seen the episode before. Sighing, Alice got up and went back to her foamie, her home base. She got out her book. She'd finished it last night, and it was the only one she had. Alice wished for the keys to the kingdom again, but Jean-Michel was worried that the books might get stolen or wrecked with so many people in the shelter, so he wouldn't let her go down to the bookstore any more. Alice put the book away. She didn't feel like rereading it.

She pulled out Juniper and hugged him. She'd felt lonely all of her life. She'd always thought it was because people kept themselves apart from her. Now she was in the middle of this huge crowd of people and she felt even more lonely. Was it because she was keeping herself apart from them?

THE PHONE WAS RINGING. Sophie didn't wait to pull off her boots. She ran right across the kitchen floor, leaving muddy footprints everywhere.

"Allo, bonjour?"

"Sophie, it's Uncle Pete. Can I talk to your Papa?" Uncle Pete didn't sound too good.

"He's in the barn," replied Sophie breathlessly. "Wait a minute and I'll take him the cordless."

Sophie ran across the drive to the barn. Too bad she couldn't talk and run at the same time. Had Uncle Pete found Alice?

Sophie thrust the phone towards Papa's hand. "It's Uncle Pete!" she whispered urgently. Sophie danced from one foot to the other while she waited for Papa to pull off his gloves and start talking.

"Henri, she wasn't there! She wasn't there! I don't know what to do! Has she called you?"

Papa told Uncle Pete to slow down. Sophie knew it couldn't be good news.

"I went to the house, and she wasn't there. There's no note. She always leaves me a note! That's our rule! The place has been looted, Henri. Windows are all broken, TV and computer gone. I checked the neighbour's house – our tree smashed through her roof and she's gone too. Alice had nobody to run to! Did the vandals take her? Why would they? Where did she go?"

Sophie could hear Uncle Pete's voice. He was practically shouting, and she could tell he was almost crying. Sophie tugged on her Papa's sleeve. She held out her hand for the phone. Papa frowned at her, but handed it over.

"Uncle Pete, Sébastien came up with an idea. He said to call the Red Cross. They manage the shelters, and if she went there, they'll probably have a list! We were going to call ourselves as soon as we were done milking. The Red Cross will find her, Uncle Pete, don't you worry."

Papa took the phone back. "It's a good idea, Pierre. Do as Sébastien says. And call us regularly. If Alice gets to a phone, she'll call us."

Papa ended the call. He took Sophie into his arms and hugged her tight.

ALICE REMEMBERED DAD'S CRANK RADIO. She was sure she'd put it into her pack. Finding it, she cranked vigorously, then wiggled into her sleeping bag. She tuned the radio to a station that played only music, no news. She didn't want to listen to any more news. Cuddling Juniper close, she put the radio beside her pillow and willed the music to take her away. Away from the noise and the smell and the worry and the loneliness.

Alice closed her eyes. She pretended she was skating, outside in the crystal fairyland that was

Montréal. Nobody was watching her. Alice wanted to keep skating all day. Then Sophie walked into her daydream. She had on skates too, and she was slipping every which way. Then she fell on her *derrière*. The daydream Alice laughed. So did Sophie, as she reached out for Alice's hand to pull her up.

All of a sudden they weren't outside any more, but shopping in the mall. Just hanging out. They saw a photo booth and decided to get their pictures taken. They were silly; everybody's silly in a photo booth. They laughed some more. It felt so good. If only Sophie were here! If only she could talk to Soph, she would feel so much better.

Alice sat straight up. She was such an idiot. She *could* talk to Sophie – the shelter had phones! Assuming, of course, that Soph's phone was working. It was worth a try. You had to wait in a long line to get your turn, but lots of people were making calls. Alice had put the phone out of her mind. Her cell was dead and Dad's cell was dead, so she'd stopped thinking about it. Alice turned off the radio, got out of the sleeping bag and marched over to join the phone line. How could she have been so dense?

"ALLO, BONJOUR?"

"*Bonjour,* Sébastien. Can I talk to your papa?"

"Sure, Uncle Pete," replied Sébastien seriously. He handed the phone over.

"Has she called yet?"

"No, Pierre," replied Papa. "Not yet. Have you contacted the Red Cross?"

"Yes," replied Pete wearily. "She was taken to a shelter downtown. But that shelter had to be moved, so they're trying to find out where she went next. I thought I would check with you, just in case."

"If she was taken by the Red Cross she will be fine, you know that, Pierre," said Papa firmly. "Keep calling. Are you still on your cell?"

"I'm not leaving the Red Cross post until I find something out. They're letting me charge my cell phone while I wait, so you can call me at that number."

"*D'accord*. We'll phone if she calls."

Uncle Pete hung up. Papa gave a deep sigh. *"Ma petite Alice,"* he said quietly. "Where are you?"

THE LINEUP WAS TEN MILES LONG. At least. Now that Alice knew she was close to talking with Sophie, or Sébastien, or *Tante* Evie or Uncle Henri — anybody who loved her — she wanted it right now. She just couldn't wait. Slowly, slowly, the line shortened. Finally it was her turn. Alice dialed the number she knew so well.

"Allo, bonjour?" came an anxious voice.

"Soph, is that you? It's me, Alice!"

Alice could hear shrieking on the other end of the line. "Soph?"

Then it was *Tante* Evie. "Alice, Alice, are you all right?"

"Of course, *Tante* Evie. Well, sort of. I don't want to be here at the shelter, I want to be with you!" Alice just blurted it out.

Then it was Uncle Henri. *"Ma petite,* where are you? Your dad is so worried!"

"I'm at Place Ville-Marie. I was at the Eaton Centre, but the ice kept falling and it was so scary. Uncle Henri, soldiers came to my house! They made me and Mrs. Hartley leave even though I didn't want to because Dad wouldn't be able to find me, but they made us because Mrs. Hartley was old and sick and hurt from where I pulled her out of her house after the tree fell on it!" Alice stopped to catch her breath. "You say my dad is worried – you've talked to him? Is he okay? I've been so worried too!"

Uncle Henri was so relieved he laughed out loud. "We have all been worried, *ma petite,* but everything is fine now, *c'est vrai?* I will call your dad and tell him where you are. Now here is Sophie. Please, talk to her before she explodes!"

Sophie grabbed the phone. "Alice, we were crazy with worry! When the bridges closed, we thought you were with your dad and he thought you were with us, so when he called we all just about went nuts!"

Just hearing Soph's voice made Alice feel warm inside. "I have so much to tell you," she said.

"Me too," replied Sophie. "You have to get here to the farm. You have to, right away. Papa won't let me talk any longer because he wants to call your dad. *Come right now!*"

Alice couldn't talk any longer either, because the guy behind her in line was starting to tap his watch. It didn't matter, Alice felt so good. Why hadn't she thought of the phone before? And now she had something useful to do with her day. Alice handed the phone to the impatient man behind her and marched back down to the end of the line. She would stand in line for another turn to call Sophie. Then another, and another, until she could leave the shelter. Now, *that* was being productive.

It wasn't so bad, waiting in line. Alice had never understood it when she heard about people waiting all night to get concert tickets and stuff but now she did. It was the goal that counted. It made the waiting almost pleasant, knowing that at the end you would get exactly what you wanted. And what she wanted was to talk to her family.

Three lines later, Alice had told Sophie about Mrs. Hartley and the tree and the pills and the muffins. Sophie had told Alice about the generator and the Mennonites and the sugar bush and Sébastien's chart. Next call, Alice was going to talk about the *Lotto-Douche*. But just as she reached the head of the line, Alice stopped in her tracks when she heard a familiar voice. She whirled around.

"Daddy!" she cried, running to the entrance and throwing herself into his arms. They held on to each other as if they never wanted to let go.

"I was so worried," Dad whispered into her hair. "I couldn't find you!"

"Oh, Daddy, I've been just fine. You didn't have to worry about me," replied Alice. "But what about you? I was worried too! Are you okay? Did you get my note?"

"What note?" said Dad as they found a couple of chairs. "There wasn't a note. All this time I thought you were at the farm, having fun with Sophie. And I finally got to a live phone last night and called to talk to you because I missed you, and that's when I found out you weren't there. I just about went mad and raced home and there was no note. Alice, that's our rule! Our special rule so we never lose each other!"

Alice hugged her Dad as tight as she could. She had never doubted that he loved her, but she'd never been so sure as she was today.

"I'm so sorry, Dad," said Alice. "I did leave a note. I know that's our rule. Didn't you find it?"

That's when Dad had to tell about the vandals. No TV, no computer. No note. Alice was sad, but not as much as she thought she'd be. Saskia had lost her whole house. Mrs. Hartley lost her roof. Sophie lost her cows. Alice felt saddest for her house, left abandoned so anything could happen to it, as if nobody cared. That was assuming a house had feelings, which was utterly ridiculous. But Alice couldn't shake the thought.

"You're safe and that's all that matters. And I'm taking you to the farm myself – so I'll know for sure you're there, safe and sound!"

To the farm, hurray! "Right now? Should I get my stuff?" Of all the things that she'd thought might happen today, going to the farm had not been on the list.

"Sorry, Princess, not yet," replied Dad. Alice frowned. "The bridges are still closed. As a matter of fact, they're asking for volunteers to knock the ice off the bridges so that traffic can start to move. I'm volunteering. Then I'm coming straight here to take you to the farm."

Alice was quiet. "Is it dangerous?" she asked in a small voice.

"No more dangerous than anything else, Princess. Who will take care of you if I get reckless on a bridge?" Dad laughed. Alice didn't. "I'll be careful, I promise." *More promises,* thought Alice.

She hated to see her dad go, but he was determined to get the job done and come back for her. After another tight hug, he was off. Alice went to take her place at the end of the phone line. She had to tell Sophie their plans.

DAY SEVEN
Sunday, January 11, 1998

THE BRIDGE

M RS. HARTLEY INSISTED ON BEING HELPED TO the big screen television in the main common room.

"This I've got to see," she said brusquely. "Foolhardy, that's what this is. Safer for us all to stay put; that ice will come down on its own eventually. What's the rush?"

Her words didn't make Alice feel any better. Foolhardy? It wasn't really, was it? Dad had said it wasn't any more dangerous than his other work. But news that a crew was going to de-ice the bridge spread quickly. Television newscasters were all over the story. "Brave heroes of the storm," they said. "Putting their lives on the line." More than anything, Alice wanted the brave hero to be somebody else's dad. Strangers at the shelter were patting her on the back and saying sympathetic things. It was making her crazy. And now they were all going to watch the spectacle together on television. Alice didn't know if she could do it.

Everyone was jostling for a good spot in front of the TV. Because Alice's father was one of the heroes, she was pushed to the very front. She was trapped. What if she couldn't stand to watch? One of the volunteers flipped through the stations. Every one was carrying the story of the bridge. The volunteer settled on CBC and put the remote down.

Some of the bridge workers were from the army. Others, like Alice's dad, were hydro linemen used to working high up in the sky. But this was higher than Alice imagined her dad had ever been. The crews climbed up the trestles, going higher and higher. They looked to be miles above the ground. One of the crews was over a stretch of highway, closed to traffic during the operation. Dad's crew was working on a section over the St. Lawrence River, frozen to a white ribbon far below them. They were all wearing bright orange survival suits and hard hats, but Alice knew right away which of the men was her dad because of the special toolbelt he wore around his waist. Her mom had given him that toolbelt.

Television helicopters circled the bridge. Every

station must have been there; there were so many of them. Some went very close to the workers. Their rotor blades kicked up all kinds of wind. *Stay away, go back,* willed Alice. *You're too close!*

But the helicopters went even closer. They pulled in for tight shots for their television audiences. Alice now could see that the men were wearing elaborate harnesses; they were roped to the bridge. *Well, of course,* she thought, feeling foolish. *A hard hat wouldn't be enough.*

Another close-up. It was Dad! He had a big hammer in his hand. The hammer was tied to his tool-belt with a rope, in case he lost his grip, Alice supposed. Mrs. Hartley reached for her hand. Alice took it gratefully. Dad raised the hammer high over his head and brought it down on the bridge. Clang! The whole structure shuddered and the sound reverberated like the largest, deepest of church bells. Clang! A chunk of ice broke away from the bridge. Clang! Another piece. Clang, clang, clang! Alice was reminded of Mrs. Hartley's window. She'd felt powerful, breaking the window with the hammer. Is that how Dad was feeling? Clang! A huge chunk of ice broke under Dad's swing and went tumbling down, bouncing off the bridge, breaking into smaller pieces, bouncing again, and then hitting the frozen river below to shatter into a thousand pieces. It was so exciting to watch. Everybody in the shelter cheered.

Alice was gripping Mrs. Hartley's hand as hard as she could. Her nails were probably digging ten little crescents into the old lady's skin, but Mrs. Hartley didn't stop her. She squeezed right back. The helicopters went in closer and closer. *Too close,* thought Alice. *Go back!* The crowd in the common room leaned forward, riveted on the screen.

It was clear that the wind from the helicopter rotors was buffeting the men on the bridge. They were trying to hold on. But it was so icy! One of the men waved the copter off. Even on TV you could tell what he was shouting. *Go back! Go back!*

And the helicopter did move back, but it was too late. The man slipped. Alice went white. Was it Dad?

It wasn't. It couldn't be. Every eye was on the falling man until all of a sudden he jerked to a stop. Then he dangled, hundreds of feet above the frozen river. It was his safety line. The line held him, just like it was supposed to! Everyone in the shelter let out their breath at the same time, and that made them all laugh with relief.

"*Aïe! Il blessera demain,* bruises for him tomorrow," said one man.

"Better than not having a tomorrow," replied another. There were nods of agreement throughout the room.

Alice turned to Mrs. Hartley, her eyes bright with tears. "It wasn't him," she whispered. "It wasn't Dad."

Mrs. Hartley smiled back.

AFTER THAT, A POLICE HELICOPTER FORCED all the television helicopters back. The shots got farther away and were less exciting to watch. Some of the crowd in the common room began to drift away. "God job, good job," they murmured to one another, just as if it were all finished now that they had lost interest. Alice found she couldn't pull her eyes away. If she did, she was afraid her dad would fall while she wasn't looking. The crews on the bridge continued to bang their hammers until they had dislodged the most dangerous pieces. The sun would take care of the rest. Alice kept watching until her dad was back on the bridge deck. She kept watching as he took off his gloves and took a hot cup of coffee from a policeman. She kept watching until he looked straight at the camera and waved. She waved back to the television set. That was for her, she knew it.

WHEN DAD WALKED THROUGH THE DOOR of the shelter, everybody applauded. Alice raced over to give him a big hug. "Now can we go to the farm?" she asked.

Dad took her small hand in his big one. "No, Princess, not yet." Alice's face fell. "It's nearly dark. Driving is incredibly treacherous and I don't want to make the trip in the dark." Dad let out a big sigh.

"And I have to admit to being a little tired."

If anybody had a right to be tired, it was Dad, thought Alice. One more day didn't matter, now that they were together. She took Dad to her foamie and let him use her sleeping bag. He was asleep in a minute. The shelter director found another one for her, and she laid it out beside him. But before she lay down, she joined the line for the phone one last time.

DAY EIGHT
Monday, January 12, 1998

W HAT'S THE HURRY, GIRL?"
Alice stopped short. She'd wanted to say goodbye to Mrs. Hartley, but now she wondered. Could she leave her? Should she?

"My dad's ready to go. He's taking me to my cousins' farm."

"About time, too," huffed Mrs. Hartley. "Leaving his own daughter to fend for herself in an emergency. Hmmph. He needs to take better care of you."

"He takes care of me just fine," Alice shot back indignantly. "We take care of each other. And it's a good thing he didn't take me away before, because you'd still be stuck under a tree!"

Mrs. Hartley grinned, which looked a little evil since she didn't have her false teeth in. "That's the spirit, girl. Fight back!"

Alice was confused. Mrs. Hartley was like two different people in one wrinkled bag of skin. Sometimes she was nice and sometimes she went back to being the Tickle Lady, nails or no nails.

"Mrs. Hartley, I want you to come with me. Aunt Evie can look after you, and I know she wouldn't mind. They don't have power, but they've got a wood stove to keep us warm and cook food and stuff. Nobody would steal your medicine there. It would be way better than this place."

Mrs. Hartley gave Alice a hard look. "You've done enough looking after me, girl," she said brusquely. "I don't like to be beholden. Go on, go to your cousins. I'm fine here, don't you worry about me." Mrs. Hartley rolled over on her side. She didn't say goodbye.

Alice sighed and picked up her stuff. That was one weird old lady. The craziest part was that Alice was actually starting to like her. She headed off to find Rachel. They'd promised to exchange phone numbers to stay in touch, assuming anybody ever had phone service again. Then Alice was ready.

"Is the car downstairs?" she asked her Dad as they rode down the elevator.

"No," replied Dad. "We're taking this." Alice started to laugh. Parked outside on St. Catherine Street was Dad's big hydro truck. "Now that's transportation!" she laughed.

"It's the safest thing," said Dad. "I've arranged to

171

work in the Triangle of Darkness for the next couple of days. That's why I'm allowed to take the truck down there."

"What's the Triangle of Darkness?" asked Alice curiously.

"It's the area around the farm. It's like a war zone down there, Princess. And I'm afraid they won't get power back for weeks."

Driving across the bridge to the South Shore was like traveling from darkness into light. It sure didn't look like a "Triangle of Darkness" to Alice, at least not in the daytime. The other side of the bridge was like a fairyland. Every house, every tree, every pole, every mailbox and every car was coated in ice. The sun sparkled on the ice, making the whole world intensely beautiful, full of diamonds and crystals. Strange ice sculptures sat in people's yards. Alice and Dad made a game of guessing what was under them. That one was a bicycle, that one a birdbath.

But under the shimmering ice also lay the twisted and shattered corpses of homes, animals and the power grid. It was a cruel fairyland.

Alice had to remind herself that the sparkling ice was killing people. It was killing animals and making people sick. It was closing schools and burning down houses. How could it do that when it was so very beautiful? Alice felt very confused, and not just about the ice storm.

"Dad, I've been thinking," she began.

"That sounds serious," teased Dad.

Alice nodded solemnly. "It is."

Dad took a deep breath. "Okay, I'm ready. Lay it on me, Princess."

"I don't want to skate competitively any more."

The words dropped like stones into a pond. They were heavy. Alice could see that Dad was thinking about how their lives would change if she didn't compete any more. After all, every single thing they did was organized around her skating.

Finally Dad said something. "But you have so much talent. Do you really want to throw it away?"

"No, I love skating more than anything," said Alice quietly.

"Well, now I'm confused." Dad sounded a little frustrated. "Do you want to skate or don't you?"

"I want to *skate*. I don't want to compete," replied Alice. "I know you're my biggest fan, Dad, but even you have to admit that I'm a lousy competitor. I get so upset before I go on that I throw up. Then I fall apart. I mop the ice on almost every jump, jumps I've done a million times in practice. You know what's it's like!"

Dad said nothing.

Alice was getting revved up. "And I'm so tired of all the TV announcers talking about my 'potential' and how I'm not living up to it. About how my 'career' is such a disappointment. I'm twelve, Dad, I'm too young to have a career!" Mrs. Hartley's words echoed in Alice's head.

Dad still said nothing.

"And what I really, really hate is that I don't have any friends. I don't have time to make any. And even if I had some, I don't have time to do anything with them. I can't go to their house after school or join the track team with them. I can't go to the mall and hang out. By the time I get home from practice, it's too late to even call anybody. Daddy," pleaded Alice. "I want to have some friends!"

Dad lifted his eyebrows. "One of the reasons your mom and I put you in skating was so that you *wouldn't* have time to hang out," he said mildly.

"Well, it's not like I want to make a career of that either. It would just be nice to do it sometimes."

Dad was quiet for a whole lot of kilometres. Finally he sighed. "So you want to quit?"

"No, not really," replied Alice. "I thought I did at first. Competitive figure skating is kind of all or nothing. But then I was talking to Mrs. Hartley and she said that when you're twelve, nothing is all or nothing. Everything is possible. So I started to think about how I could skate some of the time, just not compete."

"And what did you figure out?"

"Well," Alice took a deep breath, "I was thinking I could coach." She hurried to explain. "Not like a real pro or anything, but like a helper. I could work with the little kids on Saturday afternoon. Teach them how much fun skating can be. And teach them right, so they get good edges and control, so they build their strength up properly, like I was taught. That way I could still skate, sort of, but only on Saturday afternoons. And..." Alice took a deep breath. "If Mr. Osborne says I can, I'm going to ask him if I can keep doing one freeskate a week. Just for exercise, of course. Just so I don't forget."

Dad went quiet again. It didn't really matter what he said now. She'd told him, and that was the main thing. And it felt good. Really good. Alice waited.

A few more kilometres went by. Dad looked at Alice sideways for a second.

"Princess, you've told me what you don't like about skating. I need to know what you do like about it."

That was easy. "I love how fast I can go and I love the power I feel in my legs when I do back crosscuts. I love the solid feeling you get when you land a jump and you're perfectly centered. I love to skate when nobody's watching, when I'm doing it just for me.

"And I love it because Mom loved it."

Dad nodded his head. "I thought as much," he said softly.

They were nearing Saint-Hyacinthe. Alice recognized the farms on the outskirts. Dead animals were piled in fields. Alice couldn't help but catch her breath. Her dad was looking at the twisted hydro pylons along the highway. The landscape wasn't pretty any more. Maybe Sébastien's *loup-garou* had come to town, waged war and transformed the South Shore into a battlefield.

"Alice, we're nearly there. You don't have to skate if you don't want. So don't worry. But you've given me a lot to think about, so can we finish the talk later?"

Alice nodded. "Of course, Dad, there's other stuff to think about right now, I know that. But Dad?" Dad glanced over at her. "Thanks for listening. We don't have to decide anything right now, but I feel a lot better now that you know."

Dad smiled at her. "We're a team, Princess."

Alice gave a small smile. "You don't have to call me Princess any more, Daddy."

Dad raised his eyebrows. "I thought you liked it," he said. "When you were little you kept looking for your crown."

Alice's smile turned into a grin. "So you made me one out of tinfoil! I remember. But Daddy," said Alice earnestly, "I'm not little any more."

Dad looked sideways at her. "So, you're all grown up now?"

"Well, mostly."

Dad snorted. "We'll see about that."

Dad turned into the lane that led to the farm. Alice looked around, wide-eyed. The little shelter Uncle

Henri had built for the kids at the school bus stop was crushed to kindling. The lovely poplar trees that lined the lane were bent so low you could see over them, opening up the landscape. Alice could see for miles, she could even see the silos from the road. Dad rounded a corner and the house came into view.

Alice loved the house. Uncle Henri's grandfather had built it himself. It was white clapboard with forest green shutters. It looked like it had weathered the storm just fine except for all the icicles hanging from the roof, and there was a comforting trail of smoke coming from the stovepipe over the kitchen. But it looked empty.

Dad parked the car. He and Alice slipped and slid over the icy drive and pushed open the kitchen door. "Anybody home?" yelled Alice. "We're here!"

There was no answer. Alice went to the mudroom and found her hook. She had a hook and a set of barn clothes of her very own. She was very proud of them. It meant she belonged.

"They're probably in the milking parlour," said Alice. "I've got my own clothes, but Dad, here are some of Uncle Henri's. You can borrow them. He won't mind." They pulled on the barn clothes and headed out the back door. The noise was terrible as they got closer to the barn. "That doesn't sound good," said Alice in a worried tone. "The cows aren't supposed to be bawling like that!"

"Alice! Alice!" Sophie came running out of the barn. "You made it!"

Alice hugged her. "Is everything okay?" she asked. "I've never heard that noise before!"

"It wasn't, but it is now," said Sophie. "We just got a generator from the army. The cows are desperate. Come on, we can't stop. We have to help. Hurry!" Sophie grabbed Alice's hand and pulled her towards the barn. Dad followed behind. The grown-ups exchanged smiles and waves but they couldn't stop working. The cows needed them. Alice helped Sophie hose down the cows and clean the teats, and Dad did his best to help Sébastien with the water pump and the alley scraper. Luckily Dad wasn't too worried about getting ordered around by a nine-year-old, because Sébastien just couldn't help himself.

Compared to regular milking, the process took a long time. Compared to ice storm milking, it was a dream come true. The generator was theirs alone. They didn't have to share. They could get all the chores done in the proper order and nobody cared how long it took. But finally, finally the cows were happy. They were fed, they were watered, they were milked and the whole family felt like cheering except they were too tired.

As they trooped back to the house, Sophie's mother said, "Showers for everybody! Before you collapse!" Sébastien drew up a schedule, putting himself last. "It's been kind of nice not having to take baths," he admitted to his uncle. "Maybe the hot water will be gone before it's my turn."

It felt so good to be clean. Alice hadn't showered for six days, Dad for seven. Her aunt heated up one of her delicious casseroles in the wood stove and they sat together for a family supper. There were tired grins on everybody's faces.

"How long can you stay, Pierre?" asked Uncle Henri.

"I can stay the night. I'm working nearby for a couple of days, then going back to Montréal. I told Hydro I had to get Alice to safety before I did anything else. Thanks so much for taking care of her."

"*C'est rien,*" replied Uncle Henri. "You are both family."

"Uncle Pete," asked Sébastien, "they say we won't get power back for weeks. That can't be true, can it?"

"It is, I'm afraid," sighed Alice's dad. "Here's the problem. Some years ago Hydro-Québec built three major dams in James Bay. Most of our power comes from those dams."

"James Bay is a long way away," mused Sébastien.

"Yes, Sébastien. So how do you get all the power that Montréal needs from such a long way away? They had to design special high voltage lines that could carry more power than any line had ever carried before. These lines carry so much power that you don't need as many of them."

Everybody was nodding. That made sense. Alice's dad went on. "That means there are only five power lines feeding Montréal. By Friday, four of them had collapsed. There is only one line left to power the whole city."

"Whoa. Good thing that one didn't go!" said Sébastien.

"It's more than that," said Alice's dad seriously. "If we lose that last line, the whole city will have to be evacuated. Shut down completely. Not only does that create the problem of where to put three million homeless people, but it would take months to get the power grid operational again. Every service, like water and sewage and communications would shut down and when power came back, it would take ages to bring all the services back online, one by one. The whole economy would grind to a halt. Just think – three million people who aren't working, studying or shopping. All the businesses would close, all the schools would close and all the stores would close. Nobody would have a job. All of Canada does business with Montréal, but there would be nobody in Montréal to do any business. It's impossible to even imagine, but it nearly happened. And we're not out of the woods yet. It still could."

There was silence around the table. They had been listening to bad news for a week, but nothing this bad.

"That's why the five power lines to Montréal have to be Hydro's top priority. The grid can still fail. We can't let it. It's not that the farmers aren't important, but the safety of the grid affects everybody. That's why I have to get back to the main work in Montréal. I'm sorry, but your *'Triangle Noir'* will have to stay black for a while longer," said Alice's dad.

Sophie patted his hand. "It's not your fault, Uncle Pete. We know you're working as hard as you can. Anyway, we've got a generator now!"

"Hurray!" they all shouted. Alice's dad smiled wearily. It wasn't too much longer before Maman called bedtime. None of them had slept well for a week, since the ice storm started. Tonight everything was changed. Alice was safe, the cows were safe and the grid was safe, at least for tonight.

Sophie pulled out the trundle bed in her room and got out the comforter. She looked at it critically then pushed the trundle back under the bed. "Climb in with me," she said to Alice. "We'll stay warmer."

As Alice drifted off to sleep, she couldn't have felt happier.

Six Weeks Later

ALICE CAME OFF HER WARM-UP. MR. OSBORNE was glowering. He always glowered just before a competition. He frowned at the judges, sneered at the audience, and was grumpy with his students. As he made his way to Alice, a small smile tugged at her lip. It was time for Mr. Osborne's famous "Don't forget" speech.

"Now, Alice," he began. "Are your laces tucked in? Underwear showing? Any hairpins loose?"

"All good, Mr. O," replied Alice.

"Don't forget to keep your head up. No spaghetti arms! If the double lutz goes badly – *it doesn't matter!* Keep going. Don't hold your breath when you prepare to jump. Don't frown at me young lady, you know you hold your breath! Don't forget to smile. And remember to have *fun!*"

Remember to have fun. Mr. Osborne said it before

every competition and that was when Alice generally threw up.

Mr. Osborne had been curiously silent when she told him this was to be her last competition. Finally, he said, "I'm not giving up on you, Alice. Take a year off from competition, sure, but keep skating as much as you want. Work with the beginners on Saturdays, if it pleases you. See how you feel next year."

Then Mr. Osborne and her dad had talked for a long time. Neither one of them seemed mad, which Alice thought was a little strange. Especially after all the worrying she'd done about what they would say, about how their lives would all change.

So today she felt different. It wasn't just that her skating schedule was going to change. The ice storm had changed her too. Before the ice storm, skating was her whole life. During the storm, just surviving became way more important. And after the storm, well, Alice wasn't sure what was most important any more. Rescuing the power grid was important. It had taken thirty-three whole days, but Dad, Hydro-Québec and the linemen that came from six provinces and eight states had done it. Saving the cows was important. After Uncle Henri got the generator, not one more cow died. Other things were not quite so important. She did know that today, it didn't feel like the whole world would end if she skated badly.

Sophie was squirming on the cold arena seat. This

was always the hardest moment for her, that moment when Alice was about to go on. She looked so beautiful in her sparkly costume, standing at the boards talking to her coach. Sophie reached out and grabbed Maman's hand. Maman smiled reassuringly. Papa and Uncle Pete were talking. They both looked serious. Sébastien wasn't even paying attention to Alice. He was gazing wide-eyed at Guillaume. Sébastien had heard many stories about Guillaume the taxi driver from Alice, but she'd never told him that Guillaume knew a lot of stories about the *loup-garou*. Sébastien was mesmerized.

At the end of the row sat the Tickle Lady. Uncle Pete had collected her from the nursing home where she was staying while her roof was being repaired. Mrs. Hartley said she intended to move back next door as soon as her house could be lived in again, but that was going to take a while. So many houses needed repairs. Sophie could sure see why Alice had been terrified of her. Mrs. Hartley was fierce.

Even Alice's new friend Rachel had come with her mom. Sophie hoped having so many people there to cheer her on wouldn't freak Alice out too much. Maman had a box of Kleenex in her bag just in case.

It was time. Alice skated to her opening position and the crowd went quiet. The music began. Alice closed her eyes for a brief moment, took a deep breath and began to move.

The ice felt like it was a part of her. It was where she belonged. She barely noticed the first double-lutz, double-toe jump combination because she was flying. Alice landed so softly that she felt like the ice was cushioning her. She didn't hear the cheers of the crowd. Instead she felt the power in her thighs as she stroked hard into the double axel. She couldn't wait to lift into the air; she knew her landing would be perfect. Her footwork made her feel light as a feather and her corkscrew spin was so centered she nearly drilled a hole into the ice. Alice didn't want her solo to end. She felt just like she did in her very best practice sessions. Alice poured everything she was feeling into her final spin, threw her arms into a "V" of victory, then raised her face to the crowd. It was only when the music ended that she could hear them cheering.

Sophie's throat was raw – she'd been screaming practically non-stop since Alice began to skate. What a performance! Uncle Pete hugged Maman as tears ran down their cheeks. Guillaume had Sébastien on his shoulders so he could throw a bouquet of flowers onto the ice. Rachel and her mom were looking kind of awestruck. Only Mrs. Hartley was still sitting. She wasn't cheering or clapping or anything, but she was wearing a satisfied smile.

"Well Alice, still want to take a year off?" Mr. Osborne asked Alice gloomily at their celebratory dinner at a nearby restaurant. "Now that you're the star we always thought you could be?"

Her dad frowned at Mr. Osborne. "I know, I know," said Mr. O, putting his hands up. "No pressure. But, my girl, you certainly went out with a bang!"

Alice just smiled. "Don't worry, Mr. O. I'll be back."

THE WHOLE FAMILY WENT BACK to Alice's house. It was too late to go back to Saint-Hyacinthe, so they were having a sleepover. Anyway, they had plans. Sébastien was going to show his first-ever home movie. He was calling it a World Premiere, so Alice and Sophie dressed up like they were walking down the red carpet or something. Alice put mousse in Sébastien's dark hair, making it all spiky.

"There," she said. "Now you look like a crazy movie director."

Alice put a bag of popcorn in the microwave. Dad turned on the brand-new television, purchased just in time for the premiere. They all gathered in the living room. Sébastien put his video in the new VCR.

The movie started with a dark screen. Then Sébastien appeared, all dressed in black.

"The *loup-garou* is a shape-shifter. Mild-mannered human most of the time, at night he changes into a huge, fierce wolf. A monster. The wolf is mindless, destroying everything in its path. When it changes back to human, it has no memory of the horrors it has inflicted," he intoned in a spooky voice as he raised his arms over his head.

"I am not afraid of the *loup-garou!*" he shouted. The onscreen Sébastien made a fierce face and struck a pose. Alice covered her mouth with her hands and tried not to look at Soph. She wouldn't laugh, she wouldn't! Then the rain started.

The family was silent as they relived the storm. Sébastien had chronicled everything. He must have been carrying his video camera the whole time. He had shots of the cows bawling in the barn and of the Mennonite hand-milkers who helped. He had shots of his chart, and of the parade of neighbours who followed the travelling generator and of the lineups for the shower. Aunt Evie smiled as she saw herself organizing all the women in the kitchen to cook casseroles together.

He had filmed the wreckage of the sugar bush. He'd interviewed some of the kids at school, even some teachers, about their experiences. There were lots of stories to tell; the power had been out for thirty-three days. He even had shots of the shelter at the high school in Saint-Hyacinthe, bringing back strong memories for Alice.

But mostly, he had shots of Sophie. Sophie driving the tractor, Sophie milking the cows, Sophie feeding Mélisande, Sophie delivering the hay, Sophie hauling water, Sophie cleaning the barn, Sophie hooking up the generator. Sophie couldn't believe it. Her brother had made her look like the strongest, most capable person on earth.

When the film ended, there was silence in the living room. The movie had everything, all the laughter and all the tears. None of them would ever forget. Aunt Evie was crying, just a little, and trying to pretend she wasn't. Dad clapped his hands.

"Bravo!" he cried. "Well done!"

It broke the ice. Everybody started to talk at once, about Sébastien's cleverness, at the sneaky shots he'd been able to get when no one knew he was there, about the scary music he'd found for the soundtrack. They talked a lot about the film. They didn't talk about the ice storm. They couldn't. It *was* the monster. It had tried to destroy them. It had transformed their lives, made all of them different. But it hadn't beaten them.

Alice reached for Sophie's hand. They'd done it. They'd faced the monster, and won.

AUTHOR'S NOTE

THERE ARE TWO KINDS OF DISASTERS. THE FIRST KIND happens all at once, like an earthquake or a tsunami. Life changes in an instant. The second kind happens more slowly. It begins as an annoyance, like a leaky faucet. You try to fix the drip, but don't worry when you can't. The drip turns into a steady stream. No matter, it runs down the drain. But soon the water is pouring, gushing out of the faucet. Now you worry. As water pours onto the floor you finally realize you are in the middle of a disaster.

Some people think that slow disasters are worse than fast disasters. That's because it takes us longer to recognize that we are in trouble, and when we do, we think we have time to fix it. But we don't. A disaster is still a disaster, no matter the speed at which it occurs.

THE WEATHER

Slow disasters are often weather-related. Weather, so far, is one thing that human beings cannot control.

The ice storm of 1998 started in the sunny Gulf of Mexico. Warm, moist air floated over the tropical sea until it hit the cool edge of Alabama. The cool landmass forced the warm air to rise. Clouds formed; rain fell. The clouds moved north. It rained in Tennessee, in Kentucky, and in West Virginia. It rained in Ohio. But in Ohio, the clouds hit a wall: the Great Lakes.

It was January, winter in Canada. The warm air from the south met the cold air in the north and there was a great crash.

To escape, the warm air rose again. Clouds formed; rain formed. But it was too cold to rain. The raindrops froze into ice crystals. The crystals fell through the layer of warm air, melting back to rain. The instant the supercooled raindrops landed, they froze. They froze on the houses, on the roads, on the power lines and the trees. And that's how a whole city froze solid.

NEWS SOURCES

A great deal has been written about the ice storm. For my research, I read many newspaper articles from old copies of the *Montreal Gazette,* the *Ottawa Citizen* and the *Toronto Star.* The ice storm was breaking news for days. I also spoke to people who lived through the storm, and I visited the sugar bush and the Montreal parks that still show terrible damage from the ice. Online, you can see YouTube videos and listen to people telling about their ice storm experiences.

Want to know more, or see some pictures of the storm? There are two very good books you can check out, both edited by Mark Abley. *The Ice Storm: An Historic Record of Photographs 1998* is full of exciting, scary and heartwarming pictures. Some of the photos inspired scenes in this book. *Stories From the Ice Storm* is a collection of personal experiences. There's a whole section of stories written by kids who survived the storm. Look carefully, and you might see some ice storm stories written by your favourite authors in this book.

Whose Fault Is It? The Politics of a Disaster

When bad things happen, people have a tendency to want to blame somebody or something for all the trouble. But, the weather isn't anybody's fault.

Hydro-Québec was blamed. They were blamed for building a system dependent on only five power lines. They were blamed for not having an emergency plan and for taking so long to fix the downed lines. The fact that Hydro-Québec had also brought great wealth to the province by selling power to others while keeping rates low for Québecers was forgotten.

The Québec government was blamed for waiting three days before asking the federal government for help.

Even scientists were blamed, because they hadn't stopped climate change.

But all that blame didn't help get the power back on.

COMMUNITY

The other side of blame is praise. During the storm a wonderful sense of community developed, and from that came many happy stories.

Sixteen thousand Canadian Forces soldiers were part of *Operation Recuperation,* the largest peacetime deployment ever. They checked homes, took people to shelters, worked on the power lines, cleaned up (and recycled) the broken transformers and power lines, and distributed generators and other supplies.

When line technicians arrived in a neighbourhood to restore the power lines, homeowners applauded in the streets. They brought sandwiches, doughnuts and coffee to the workers.

Communities got together and collected winter clothes for the American line technicians who came from the warm south to help. They weren't used to working in wind chill conditions of -40 degrees Celsius, but it didn't stop them.

One hundred and forty line technicians from Manitoba drove for thirty-six straight hours to come to help in the Triangle of Darkness. The town where they were stationed flew the Manitoba flag the whole time they were there.

Lots of people contributed their personal skills. Electricians and plumbers manned open-line talk shows over the radio to help people protect their homes from damage. Doctors made house calls. Ham radio operators relayed messages between emergency personnel and hospitals. Pet stores with generators collected tropical fish and "fishsat" them to save their lives. Hairstylists visited shelters, styling hair for free to raise peoples' spirits.

Volunteers in Toronto created *Project Warmth,* collecting five hundred sleeping bags to send to the freezing people in the Triangle of Darkness.

My favourite storm story comes from a small, very poor village in Mali, Africa. For years, the dairy farmers of this village had benefited from aid from the richer farmers of Québec. When the African villagers heard of the ice storm, they sent a donation to their Canadian friends.

STORYTELLING AND THE *Loup-garou*

The Québecois have a rich cultural tradition of stories, songs and dance. The stories traveled from France with the earliest settlers, then changed to fit the needs of the New World, making them uniquely Québecois. Many of the stories are about the *loup-garou.*

"*Loup-garou*" is the French word for a man who changes into a wolf, or werewolf. However, a *loup-garou* may shift into a big black dog, a cow, a pig or a horse as well. In French Canada, the legend of the *loup-garou* was closely connected to the spiritual beliefs of the people.

If a man did not go to church on Sunday for seven years, or missed communion at Easter, it was believed that he would fall under the spell of the devil and become a *loup-garou*. The punishment lasted for 101 days and nights. During the day, the victim would be frightened and sickly. At night, he was forced to wander as an animal. The spell could be broken if someone recognized the *loup-garou* while in animal form, and was able to pierce it with a knife and draw blood. The victim would immediately become human again. But the curse could only be fully lifted if neither party spoke of it until all 101 days were up.

The other way to become a *loup-garou* was to put on a wolfskin belt. This belt gave the wearer special powers, but at a terrible cost. The curse died if the belt was burned, but so too did the victim.

Stories like these were told to children in old Québec so they would obey their parents. It's no wonder that Sébastien was frightened!

MAPLE SYRUP

Québec provides 70% of the maple syrup for the whole world. In 1998 there were nearly 28 million maple taps in Québec, and a quarter of them were damaged or destroyed. Experts say that it will take thirty to forty years for production to be restored.

Many believe that the loss of the sugar bush was the

greatest of all the losses, because it will take the longest to recover.

DAIRY FARMING

Dairy farming is a very important occupation in Québec. There are more dairy cows there than in any other province in Canada, and many live on small family farms like Sophie's.

But only 3% of the people in Canada live on a farm. That means there are a whole lot of us (like me!) who live in cities and don't know much about farming. Here are some questions that I asked dairy farmers before I wrote this book:

How much milk does a cow give each day? Cows give about 6 to 8 gallons of milk a day. But it varies. Some cows are better milkers than others, and they can produce up to 12 gallons a day.

What do cows eat? Cows eat an enormous amount of feed each day. It's a combination of hay, corn and silage, which is fermented corn or grass. And they drink a lot of water. In fact, the amount of water that a single cow drinks in a year would completely fill the inside of your school bus!

Here's how to imagine a cow's daily meal. It's a big picnic cooler filled with hay, a blue recycling box filled with grain and eight four-litre jugs of water. Could you eat all that?

How can a cow eat that much feed? A cow has a

special stomach with four chambers to help digest the feed. After a cow eats, she regurgitates a ball of partially digested food the size of a golf ball into her mouth, where she chews it about sixty times. Then she swallows it, and brings up another one. This is called "chewing the cud." A cow chews 30,000 times a day!

What does a farmer do all day? Dairy farmers and their families work very long hours. There are many chores to do as well as milking, like feeding the cows, feeding the calves and the young heifers (they get different feed), cleaning the stalls and equipment, managing the feed that goes into the silos, and growing and harvesting hay and grain to feed the animals. On top of that, many dairy farmers have other businesses as well. Some keep chickens or sheep. Some make cheese from the milk. Some work off the farm, sometimes as school bus drivers. In Québec, many make maple syrup like Sophie's family. And farmers don't get any days off, either. Cows have to eat and be milked every day, not just Monday to Friday.

Isn't a farm a dirty place? No! A dairy farm is kept very clean. Farmers wear surgical gloves just like a doctor, and wash and sanitize their equipment every single day to make sure that the milk is free from germs.

A dairy inspector comes regularly to every farm to make sure that the cows are being looked after and the equipment is clean and sanitary. These rules ensure that our milk is always safe to drink.

What does a farm do with all the manure? A dairy cow creates about 50 kilograms of manure *every day*.

But it isn't just waste. Manure can be used as a fertilizer for the fields, or as compost. Some farmers dry the manure until it looks like sawdust, and then use it as bedding for the cows. And some farmers are even exploring ways to turn their manure into power. The manure is turned into methane gas, which can then be burned to generate electricity. That would sure help in a power failure!

Computerization on a Dairy Farm Ever see a cow use a computer? Well, maybe that's a little silly, but farmers use computers for lots of things. A computer figures out the best combination of food and vitamins for each cow. A computer keeps track of how much milk a cow gives, and when it's time for her to have a new calf. On some farms, cows wear computer bracelets on their legs to count how many steps they take each day, because a healthy cow is an active cow. So, if you want to be a farmer, you have to *really* like computers.

ICE STORM TRIVIA

- Do you remember the movie *Titanic?* It's the story of an ocean liner that hits an iceberg and sinks. This movie had just come out in theatres when the ice storm hit, and many theatre-goers only got to see half of it because the power went out.

- Seven line technicians who came from New-foundland to help during the storm chipped in together to buy a Lotto ticket while they were in Québec. They won – and took home $1.89 million.

- Word of the day: the cranes that line technicians use to get up to the power lines are called "cherry pickers" in English. In French, they're called *"girafes."*

- The final numbers: here's how much power equipment had to be replaced to get electricity back up and running:
  Pylons: 1,300
  Hydro Poles: 10,750
  Insulators: 84,000
  Transformers: 1,800
  Wire/Cable: 2,800 km

For more information, as well as great sites to visit, videos to watch and games to play, check out: www.pennydraper.ca

ACKNOWLEDGEMENTS

I AM INDEBTED TO MY COUSINS, SHIRLEY AND KEN PEER of Hillandale Farms. Not only do they put milk on our table and keep our huge family in touch, they spent hours teaching me about life on a dairy farm. Any errors in the book are mine and mine alone. And to Caroline Peer: thanks for the helpful hints, and for not laughing when I grossly overestimated the number of dairy cows on a family farm!

My particular thanks go to my editor, Barbara Sapergia, who worked so hard helping me weave the disparate tales into one. I so enjoy our grammar debates, and will never look at a semi-colon the same way again!

And my most heartfelt thanks go, as always, to my family. My first readers, best critics and most patient supporters.

ABOUT THE AUTHOR

PENNY DRAPER IS AN AUTHOR, A BOOKSELLER AND A storyteller who lives in Victoria, BC. Originally from Toronto, she received a degree in Literature from Trinity College, University of Toronto and attended the Storytellers' School of Toronto. For many years, Penny shared tales as a professional storyteller at schools, libraries, conferences, festivals and on radio and television. She has told stories in an Arabian harem and from inside a bear's belly – but that is a story in itself.

Penny's books have been nominated for numerous awards in Canada and the United States. They have been honoured with the Victoria Book Prize, the Moonbeam Award Gold Medal and the Chocolate Lily Readers' Choice Award (runner-up). *Ice Storm* is part of Coteau Books for Kids *Disaster Strikes!* series. The series also includes Penny's *Terror at Turtle Mountain*, *Peril at Pier Nine*, *The Graveyard of the Sea* and *A Terrible Roar of Water*.